CW01269860

A Position in Paris
Copyright © 2018 by Megan Reddaway

Published by the author
meganreddaway.com

Cover art: Natasha Snow: natashasnowdesigns.com
Editor: Carole-ann Galloway

First edition 1.0
August, 2018

ISBN: 978-1-71810-91-93

This book is written in British English. If you're not used to reading British English, please be tolerant of variations in spelling and usage.

This is a work of fiction. Names, characters, places, and incidents are either the product of the author's imagination or are used fictitiously. Any resemblance to actual persons living or dead, businesses, events, or locales is entirely coincidental. Any persons depicted on the cover are models used for illustrative purposes only.

All rights reserved. No part of this book may be copied, reproduced, translated, or transmitted in any manner whatsoever without the written permission of the author, except for brief quotations included in reviews. To request permission and all other enquiries, contact the author at meganreddaway.com/contact

Please do not copy or share this ebook. Support your favourite books and authors by posting reviews instead, and keep the supply of good books coming!

A Position in Paris

By Megan Reddaway

1

James's Journal
Paris, Friday, December 6th, 1918

I must find something to interest me, or I shall lose my mind.

The war has taken my youth and my strength, my leg and my eye. Now it is over, and those who once applauded a hero turn away in search of more pleasant sights. The urchins of Paris point to my eye patch, my sewn-up trouser leg, and my crutches, shouting *"Le pirate! Le pirate!"* as I hobble from the street door to my carriage.

I cannot hope for love unless I pay for it. I have plenty of money, and for that I should be grateful. Yet when I see other wounded men, cripples in tattered uniforms begging in the streets, I envy them. They still have a reason to struggle.

Diana came this afternoon, and from loneliness and tedium I did the stupidest thing I have done since that hopeless charge at Reims. I proposed.

She was telling me of her two suitors. My leg bothered me—the amputation is not healing as it should—and I felt so dull that I could think of nothing to amuse her in return, so I let her run on.

"They say there is a shortage of men, but I have never had so many courting me. Bill is my natural mate, perhaps.

He would give me no unpleasant surprises. Johnny is an adventurer, who says motor cars will make him rich. He offers me more passion, but I am not sure it will last. Which of them do you think I should marry, James?"

Parkin came in to stoke the fire. He is not always so attentive to my guests' comfort, but he approves of Diana.

"Why should you marry at all?" I asked her. "A widow can do as she likes. Are you not happy as you are?"

"I want companionship and the devotion of one man."

"But you are not in love with either of them?"

"Love—what is love?" She brushed a crumb from her skirt with the cotton gloves she wears to hide hands still reddened by the ammonia of the hospital wards. "Love comes and goes. One can rely on it for three months at best. Then the honeymoon is over, and what counts in a marriage is respect. Respect and friendship."

"Then marry neither of them," I said, in a burst of nostalgia. "We are friends, and we respect one another. Marry me."

I succeeded in amusing her, at least. She tossed her head back and laughed.

"You would have married me in 1913," I said, stung.

She reached for her cigarette case. I found mine first and flipped it open for her. She let me light her cigarette, watching the flame with faraway eyes.

"Yes, you were a handsome devil," she said. "I suppose you might have enticed me up the aisle, had you tried—but we would both have regretted it."

Bitterness clouded my vision. "*You* would have regretted it, at any rate. No one could call me a handsome devil now."

She sat up straight, her eyes big with distress. "I didn't mean that! You know I didn't. And I am awfully fond of you, of course I am, in a sisterly way."

"Dear Diana. I always wished for a sister," I said drily.

She looked away from me and breathed out a ring of blue smoke. We watched it spread and distort until it vanished somewhere in front of the bookcase.

"In 1913, I didn't know what you were," she said. "We were all so innocent, and I more than most. I scarcely knew what men and women did together, let alone what men might do with other men. But I have seen a good deal since."

No doubt. And I had not pursued her, in that spring before my disgrace when we first met, because my interest had been in her brother, who had not returned it. He was dead two years later, and so was the man Diana had married.

She had taken the double bereavement hard. Soon afterwards, she had joined Queen Alexandra's Nursing Service. When we met again last summer, at the field hospital where I began to recover from my wounds, we had become two different people — two people, however, who understood each other better than our younger selves ever had.

She turned back to me. Her voice was brittle and light as she said, "I hear a dreadful young man comes calling several times a week."

"I shall end that."

"I suppose if you were respectably married, your father might relent and admit he has a second son?"

My leg throbbed. I shifted in my seat, but it did not ease. "He might, but don't count on it. I have my uncle's legacy. It would be plenty for us both. I would make you an allowance, and you would have your freedom. You could flit between your Bills and your Johnnies without having to choose one and stick to him till death do you part."

"And you? What would you gain from it?"

"Companionship, as you said? An interest in life?"

She appeared to be considering my offer, and a chill ran through me. Did I mean her to take me seriously? What should I do if she accepted? I would have a friend by my side, a trained nurse — I believe I had been thinking mostly of that.

But all was well. A moment later she reached over to stub out her cigarette in the silver tray between us, and again she laughed.

"My dear James, if you want company and an interest in life, go to every party and keep a journal."

And so I have found this book and begun.

Sunday, December 8th

Loulou came to supper last night. He is the young man to whom Diana objected. He spoke of the theatre and the liaisons of his friends, and praised the fashion houses that will break out in bright colours next year, he says, after the gloomy restrictions of the war. He mentioned how exquisite my apartment looked by candlelight and complimented me on my new waistcoat. In short, he said all the right things.

After an excellent meal and two Benedictines, accompanied by Loulou's chatter and his easy smile, I persuaded myself that his tenderness and passion were real, not the result of the thousands of francs that have passed from my hands to his. I told Parkin I did not need him: Mr. Duquesne would help me to bed.

Parkin's face was a mask. He does not like Loulou.

When Loulou left in the morning, he folded into his pocket the cheque I had given him for drawing lessons or the care of his grandmother or whatever it was this time. I turned away from the closing door and caught sight of my face reflected in the looking glass, without the patch over the empty socket—a grinning death's-head. Then I knew the truth of our relations, and a profound depression fell upon me.

I cannot think badly of Louis. It is commerce to him, and he keeps his side of the bargain. I only despise myself.

I am twenty-nine years old, and I feel sixty. No, older still—for Parkin is sixty, and there is more love in his life, and more life in his love, than in mine.

There is a tale behind Parkin's appointment. It may amuse me to tell it.

Parkin is not an old family retainer, as my visitors assume. The family retainers were retained by my family when my father cast me out. Parkin was recommended to me when I had been transferred from the field hospital to Paris and was close to being released into the world.

I could not go back to England. My father had threatened to make my life impossible if I try to settle there.

But I was fortunate to have a sympathetic great-uncle, a gracious old gentleman who had spent most of his life in Paris. Our tastes were similar, though our personalities were very different. I visited him on all my leaves until he died in 1917, bequeathing to me most of his wealth and this apartment.

The building could not be more convenient. The apartment has electric wiring and a telephone, and—most importantly for me on my crutches—there is a lift, worked by the concierge, in the shaft where the service staircase used to be. So when they let me out of the convalescent home, I installed myself here to see out the war and consult the cream of Paris's doctors.

My uncle's servants had left, pensioned off under his will, so I looked for replacements. I wanted a French cook and an English valet, if I could get them—the best possible combination. The other way around would be a disaster!

I got the cook without too much trouble. His name is Henri and, like me, he is one of the limping wounded. An English valet was harder to find until I chanced upon Parkin, who had worked from boyhood in one of the most illustrious houses in England. He consented to come to me because he wished to stay in Paris and I agreed to be flexible in the matter of "afternoons."

If I have a tea or dinner party, Parkin is always here to serve it. Otherwise, he takes one afternoon and one evening each week, on whichever days he chooses—different days every week. I do not know how late his evenings run, but he does not stay out all night. If I wake after a bad dream and ring the bell, he answers it.

This lack of routine does not disturb me. My main requirement is that he be here every morning to bring me tea, dress me, make my breakfast, and help me face the beginning of each day. That is when I cannot do without a gentleman's gentleman. At the end of the evening I do not need him so much, because it does not matter how I look. The concierge can step in, or Loulou if he is here. Nevertheless, Parkin's wish for flexibility struck me as remarkable.

"The duke did not dismiss you?" I asked at our first interview. I had his reference in front of me, but I wanted to hear it from him.

"No, sir. His Grace is returning to England, and I should prefer to stay."

This preference was so astonishing, I could not let it pass without comment. "My experience of English servants is that their dislike of 'foreign parts' amounts almost to an allergy."

"That is no doubt true in most cases, sir."

"And they prize regularity in their afternoons off above all things."

"Again, I am sure you are correct."

"And yet you wish to live in foreign parts and be irregular in your afternoons? You intrigue me, Parkin. I believe we shall get on very well."

Which we do, but I did not let the matter rest until I had discovered his secret. It is simple and rather charming. At the age of fifty-nine, he had suffered what the French call a *coup de foudre*, a lightning bolt, and had fallen in love with the English butler in the house next to the one the duke and duchess had taken on a famous boulevard. His feelings were returned, so Parkin wished to stay in Paris. The butler's employer is a well-known French nobleman, active in both government and society, and the butler has to take his time off when he can—thus Parkin's need for flexibility.

I have never seen them together, but I imagine them as a stately, respectable pair taking tea in the little attic room they might rent in Montmartre.

Yes, it has cheered me to write that. Perhaps there is something in this idea of a journal.

Thursday, December 19th

The weeks pass. I am going through torture. The new man wrenches my shoulder every day. It will become straight in time, he says.

They tried to fit a false leg, but the stump became inflamed again and would not take it.

The socket is not well-enough healed for anything to be done in the place where my eye once was.

It will be months before I see any real improvement.

I am a useless creature who should have been killed outright. I loathe myself, and Loulou, and all the world.

Saturday, December 21st

Claude made a suggestion:

"You are becoming insupportable," he said. "Either let me find you a new young man, or write a book. Your mind is as sharp as a razor, and it needs activity, or it will injure you and all your friends."

I was sceptical at first, thinking Claude was simply tired of me. He is the only one who can discuss art with me with any degree of intelligence, and I have asked a lot of him in the last few months. Writing a book would keep me quiet and take me off his hands.

But is it such a bad idea? I could write a novel, perhaps. A war story? No, people do not want that now. They want to read about love and dancing... but writing about love and dancing would make me unutterably sad.

Not a novel, then.

Something philosophical?

Or a book about art — about chinoiserie? Yes, that might be the thing. My uncle left me his collection of eighteenth-century imitations of Chinese lacquer and porcelain with the apartment. I have picked up more and become quite an expert.

Claude could lend me any reference books I need. I shall tell him he must also find me a secretary, a good shorthand typist. I do not wish to write in French, so he will have to track down a British one, or an American. A woman would be best. If it is a man, he must not be of the Loulou type. In my dependent state I should be easy prey.

Paris seems full of English-speaking voices, so he should not have too much trouble. People are flooding back. A crowd of them come to play bridge and chatter to each other in my apartment several times a week.

"Everyone has returned to Paris now," they told me today. "Last year was so difficult, with the bombs and the influenza! One would bury oneself in the country until one felt so dull that death lost its sting, then return to Paris until fear overcame boredom, and back to the country again. Now everyone is in Paris, nonstop. Such a relief."

"Then the epidemic has ended?" I asked.

"They say the worst is over. Anyway, it has spread to the country, so one may as well stay in Paris, where at least one can have an agreeable time."

Diana is not in this circle. The nurses, like the men who have fought, do not speak so lightly of death.

Society is split in two. On one side are those who saw action and the truly bereaved. On the other, those who kept clear of the blood and mud. I do not know how I have become associated with the second type. I suppose my money attracts them, and I do not care enough to send them away. Anything is better than being always alone or with others as scarred as myself.

Friday, January 3rd, 1919

I see I have written nothing since before Christmas. I have no wish to describe all the parties, so I shall leave it thus.

Claude sent me a potential secretary today—a loud, bouncing, jolly woman of fifty, like the worst kind of medical nurse. She had not been in the apartment five minutes before I was longing to throw her from the windows. Fortunately, at the end of the interview she admitted she could only offer afternoons.

I rang for Parkin to show her out before she had finished speaking. Then I telephoned to tell Claude it was no use sending me people with such limitations.

He feigned innocence. "I thought you would like her, *mon cher*. She is not at all like Louis."

"Louis be damned. You have not understood my requirements. I must have three full days—either Monday, Wednesday, and Friday, or Tuesday, Thursday, and Saturday. On the days my secretary comes, I will dictate in the morning. In the afternoons I may have engagements, or I may need to rest. She can spend that time typing from her shorthand notes. The following day, when she is not there, I will make corrections and plan the next section. Then she returns on the third day, and we repeat. Do you see?"

"Yes, but if you are so precise in your demands, you must expect to pay a higher rate. You offer half a post while giving your employee little chance of finding anything to fill her other three days."

"Then I shall pay for a full week. Money is not a barrier. I must have the person at my beck and call. And, Claude—please find someone *quiet*."

2

Edmund's Journal (in shorthand)
Paris, Monday, January 6th, 1919

A clear, cold day. Robby seems better. He is out of bed and reading one of his storybooks.

Madame H. reminded me that our rent was overdue. I asked for more time, but she shrugged in the French way and said, "It is not difficult to find tenants, monsieur. Every house is full since the war ended."

It is true. I have looked for cheaper rooms and can find nothing respectable. One sees in the streets how the population has swelled since the armistice. It is a different city from the Paris of shortages and bombardments that we came to last summer.

So I gave her another portion of the Red Cross money that was never quite enough to take us to Switzerland.

I suggested to Mama that I might share Robby's room to reduce the rent, but she would not hear of it, so I agreed to leave things as they are for now. I think, though, that we must do something of the kind if nothing turns up by the end of this month.

She showed me Charles's suit, all cut about. She talks of becoming a dressmaker and, for practice, she is altering it to fit me. I wish she had not begun. A well-made suit from before the war might have fetched a good price.

The peace conference begins in two weeks, and it must employ clerks. How does one apply? I shall write to Mrs. Bullock. She may be able to advise me.

Thursday, January 9th

A note from Mrs. Bullock awaited me at the stationer's. She could not help with the conference except to suggest that I try the British embassy, which I should prefer not to do. They would want to see official papers.

However, she enclosed a letter of recommendation to a French acquaintance at the Académie des Beaux-Arts, who is acting on behalf of an English gentleman seeking a secretary. I called on the Frenchman at once, and he has given me an appointment for an interview at the Englishman's apartment tomorrow.

It seems a strange way to go about things, and I fear I recognised something in the Frenchman's manner — something that both draws and repels me. He was effusive in his compliments on my French, seemed delighted at my youth, and hinted that an attractive appearance would help me secure the post. Six weeks ago I might have backed away, but we are in such straits now that I cannot turn down any opportunity lightly.

I shall wear Charles's suit and the tinted glasses that Robby's last nurse left behind, in order to look as dull and businesslike as possible.

I have not told Mama, in case it involves some immorality and I have to refuse.

3

James's Journal
Friday, January 10th

The first step on my path to authorship is taken. I have appointed a secretary. I am as pleased with myself as if I had already written the book!

It is a young man, but a very quiet one, thin and plain and pale. He is poor, I think. His clothing was tailored but designed for a bigger man and imperfectly altered.

From his speech and manner I should have said he was from a good English family, but the little he told me of his background suggests the dullest bourgeois life. However, he seems efficient, and he came with an excellent reference from the lady in charge of the Paris office of the American Red Cross.

He has a firm but delicate jawline, a sensitive mouth, and two eyes, I assume. I cannot be sure about the eyes because he wore the ugliest pair of horn-rimmed dark glasses I have ever seen.

I attempted a joke about them. "I wear one eye patch. You appear to wear two."

His brows drew together. "What do you mean?"

"Will you not take off your glasses?"

"No, I—" He flushed. "My eyes are weak."

"Then should you be straining them with secretarial work?"

"There is no difficulty with that. It is only bright lights."

He is a poor liar, but I did not press him. He may have some deformity. I would not be pleased if people asked me to remove my eye patch to satisfy their curiosity.

Along with the reference, he handed me a paper on which he had typed the abbreviated facts of his life. I did not give it more than a glance at the time, but I have it here, and it is astonishing in its lack of information.

Name: E. Vaughan. No Christian names.

Birth: October 1897. No day or place.

Employment, 1915-18: Bank clerk (no name or address of the employer). *August to November 1918: American Red Cross, Paris*, followed by a list of his duties there.

There is no personal address in Paris, although if he has been here since August, he must have one.

What is his first name, I wonder? Edward seems most likely, or Eustace, perhaps. Ernest? I hope not. I do not see him as an Ernie. Ernie is a chirpy chap, calling "Cheerio!" as he marches off to the front with Tommy, Alf, and Bert. So many of them passed through the ranks of my battalion on the way to oblivion. He is not at all that type.

I asked where he was educated, and he told me Friern Barnet Grammar School. A red-brick establishment, no doubt, crowded with the sons of prosperous shopkeepers and poor clergymen. That is perhaps his background — the son of a meek and mild vicar.

"Why were you not in the war?" I asked.

"I was not required to serve."

I did the arithmetic and could see no reason for it. He was old enough, and weak eyes would not have excused him. A man who was medically unfit would have been given a desk job or some other war work, unless severely disabled. A conscientious objector would have been in the Non-Combatant Corps, in prison, or in a work camp. Neither the unfit nor the conchie could have worked as a bank clerk or come to live in Paris last summer.

"Why was that?"

He seemed unwilling to reply, as if I were dragging his history from him under torture. Finally he admitted, "I was born in Ireland, in Belfast. I was living there."

"And the Irish were not conscripted. I see. But you did not go to school in Ireland. Friern Barnet is on the fringes of London, is it not? Was it a boarding school?"

Another hesitation. "No, I grew up in London."

"And moved to Ireland to escape conscription?" Resentment prickled at me, as it always does when I come upon able-bodied men who escaped the battlefields.

"No." He flushed red. "I took a job there as soon as I left school, in the summer of 1915."

"A few months before conscription was introduced in England. There was talk of it, perhaps?"

He answered stiffly, "If there were rumours, I did not hear them."

In the army I learned to tell a truthful man from a liar, and he appeared to be speaking the truth. My resentment faded. In any case, I did not feel as I had with the female—I was not looking for reasons to be rid of him. He seemed acceptable, I was eager to start the book, and Claude had proposed no other candidates.

I glanced at his sheet of paper. "It was in Belfast that you worked in a bank, then? Do you have a reference from that employer?"

A frown line appeared on his forehead, and he shifted in his chair. "No. I wanted to come to Paris, and they gave permission at first, but... in short, I stayed away longer than they liked, and I was dismissed."

I did not mind his having been dismissed for that reason. They had clearly valued him if they wanted him back so much. Besides, if I attempted to become a bank clerk, I am sure I would be dismissed on the first day. However, I wrote down *Belfast, no reference* because making a note seemed the thing to do.

"Let us move to a practical demonstration of your skills."

I gave him the same test I had inflicted on the woman. He took out a notebook and pencil — he had come well equipped — and I dictated.

"In the eighteenth century, the fascination of well-to-do Europeans with the art and culture of China led to a surge in demand that could not be met with genuine Chinese artefacts. People wanted Chinese plates, Chinese wallpaper, Chinese lacquer cabinets, or something approaching their idea of them. European artists stepped in to produce whatever was required, and chinoiserie was born." I continued in this vein for a few more paragraphs. His pencil halted a couple of seconds after I stopped. "That will do. If you would be so good as to come through and type it out..."

I made my halting way to the double doors leading from the salon to the library. The typewriting machine stood gleaming upon the table. He followed me and sat at the desk, then rolled in a sheet of paper. But he hesitated with his hands over the keys, frowning.

It did not take a genius to see there was a problem, so I asked with some irritation, "What is it? Is anything wrong with the machine? I have it on approval, so I can get another if this one is not fit for the purpose."

His face cleared, and his shoulders relaxed. "The typewriter is a good one. It is only a question of the layout of the keys. They are arranged according to the frequency of use of each letter, you see, so the machines are assembled differently for every language. This is a French machine, while I have learned on one designed for English. The *A* and *Q* are reversed, the *M* is here instead of here, the *W* . . . the *Z* . . ."

As he talked he became animated. The icy mask melted, and his personality shone through. I believe he is not cold at all, but passionate, earnest, and sensitive. I was fascinated — by him, not by the history of typewriting machines — and I determined to employ him at any cost.

"So you cannot use it?" I asked, when he finished his explanation.

"I can, but there may be mistakes at first. I will try it now and show you. In a week or two I would adapt to it, no doubt, but it will always be slower for typing in English because the keys are more likely to lock. If you can change the machine without expense . . ."

"I shall instruct them at once."

He tore a page from his notebook and wrote three lines of letters. "This is how it should be. If you can get a British layout, it will have the pound sterling symbol up here with the numbers. That will be useful if you will be referring to values in pounds. The American layout has only the dollar, but otherwise it is the same, so it would do very well. I could leave a space and handwrite the sterling symbol where necessary."

The female candidate had told me none of this.

I left him to his typewriting and waited with some impatience in the salon. He brought me the transcript a few minutes later. It was flawless.

"Thank you, Vaughan. You seem suitable for the post. Shall we discuss the salary?"

I named the figure I had in mind. He did not answer at once. His Adam's apple bobbed as he swallowed.

"Is it not enough?" I asked.

He cleared his throat. "It seems too much for three days. It is more than I earned for a five-and-a-half-day week during the war, when salaries were higher."

Yes, he must be the son of a clergyman. Nobody else would be so self-destructively truthful.

"I have been told I must pay the full week if I want you always available. I would prefer that you do not take other employment on the intervening days, in case I have engagements that require a rearrangement of your hours. Do you accept the post at this rate of pay or not?"

He hesitated for another moment, then said, "I do. Thank you. I shall do my best to merit it."

Vaughan had suggested I should telephone the Red Cross to verify his reference. When he had left, I did so, not because I suspected any forgery, but to ask why they had let this apparently perfect employee out of their grasp. Mrs.

Bullock—whom I believe I have met, probably at Diana's—assured me she had not wanted to lose him, but so many former servicemen and nurses wished to live and work in Paris after the armistice that she had been obliged to replace him with an American.

"What did you think of him, Parkin?" I asked as I replaced the receiver. He had passed me in the hall and must have caught the end of the conversation.

"I couldn't say, sir, but if you have employed the young gentleman, I trust he will suit."

Parkin never gives his opinion plainly. This may not sound like high praise, but the clue is in the word *gentleman*. Parkin approves.

Loulou is never anything but "the young man" to Parkin. I have tried to get him to say "Mr. Duquesne" or even "Mr. Louis," and he inclines his head as if agreeing but does not do it. Loulou retaliates by referring to Parkin as "your servant." How do they address each other face-to-face? Perhaps they never do.

Why do I compare Vaughan and Louis in this way?

I suppose I must call him "Vaughan." I could not call him anything else aloud, but if I knew his Christian name, I could use it privately in this journal.

I could have asked Mrs. Bullock. She must know it. But I would prefer to find it out for myself, along with his other secrets, as I did Parkin's. It will amuse me to open him up inch by inch.

4

Edmund's Journal
Friday, January 10th

I am now Private Secretary to The Honourable Lieutenant Colonel J. B. V. Clarynton, VC!

I start next Thursday, when he hopes to have the new typewriter. He gave me an advance of two weeks' salary, which he said was a retainer to stop me taking a position elsewhere in the meantime — as if that were likely!

He kept asking about Belfast. It was disconcerting, since I have nothing to hide in that respect. I did not go there to escape conscription. I never dreamed the government might take men who had not volunteered.

It is true that I did not want to fight, although I would have done my duty if I had been called up. My soul rebels at the thought of shooting another man. Colonel Clarynton saw this in me, I think. However, it did not stop him from offering me the post.

I am not entirely at ease about it. The salary is far too high, and I have never heard of it being paid in advance. But he does seem to need a secretary. He tested my shorthand and typewriting, and I saw notes for the book he plans to write. He has lost a leg below the knee and gets about on crutches, so he cannot be any physical threat to me. Moreover, he has an old servant in residence, an

English valet named Parkin. I felt that I could trust Parkin, and no harm will come to me while he is there.

Mama shed tears of joy and could not stop hugging me. She has sent out for chicken fricassée. Robby does not understand how much this job means — we were careful not to let him know how precarious our situation had become — but he tells me it feels like Christmas all over again.

5

James's Journal
Thursday, January 16th

Vaughan came punctually at ten, wearing the same ill-fitting suit. I had given him a small advance on his salary, hoping he might spend it on new clothes, but no. He must have more pressing expenses.

He came into the salon to take dictation. I was full of ideas and launched into the first chapter. After an hour or so, I stopped and asked him to read it over to me. I was afraid he would be unable to decipher the squiggles he had made in his notebook, but my words were repeated faithfully back to me. It was strange to hear them in another voice!

At half past twelve, he retreated to the library. Parkin had told me I must expect to give him lunch and an hour off in which to eat it.

"What will he have?" I had asked.

"The same as you, sir."

"And what is that?"

I do not order lunch, because I do not care what I eat at midday. I leave the decision to my cook. He lost a leg at the First Battle of the Aisne, so we are in sympathy.

"Henri thought an omelette today," Parkin said.

"It will not take Vaughan an hour to eat an omelette."

"All the same, sir, I believe you will find an hour is expected."

It is the "done thing," it seems, so I must do it. It is a nuisance, but I suppose it makes little difference, as long as the work is done by the end of the day.

He went out for a walk when he had eaten. I heard the typewriter start up at half past one, and then I must have dozed. The next thing I knew, Parkin was coming in to light the lamps and draw the curtains.

"Mr. Vaughan says he's finished the work he had, and is there anything else?" Parkin said, when he saw I was awake.

"No— Yes. Ask him to bring it in, would you?"

My secretary came in and handed me a sheaf of paper. The first pages of my book! I did not read them closely—I will do that tomorrow—but I was delighted to see the neat black typescript on the virginal paper. It gave my words a weight I am sure they do not deserve!

He sat in silence while I gazed at his work. *That is good*, I thought. *He will be a soothing presence, no more trouble than a piece of furniture.*

However, he has a strong mind when roused, as I soon found.

It occurred to me to give him the name of my tailor. "You may go there and order a new suit of clothes on my account."

He frowned. "I wouldn't put you to the expense, Colonel Clarynton."

I answered in the tone in which I would have addressed an insubordinate junior officer. "Your clothes do not fit you, Vaughan. The Americans may not have noticed, but I have and my friends will, if any of them should chance to see you here. You are not a credit to me, dressed as you are. I don't mind the expense any more than I should mind paying for my own clothes. In fact, it is even more worthwhile, because I have to look at you all morning, but I rarely have to look at myself."

Two spots of colour had appeared on his cheeks, high on the bone, and he sat up straight in his chair. He clearly wished to refuse. He is a very proud young man, I think.

"Does Parkin go to your tailor?" he asked.

"No, but he has a tailor of his own and does not wear hand-me-downs."

He flinched as if I had struck him. It occurred to me, too late, that the suit might have belonged to a father or brother killed in the war. But how can I be sensitive to his circumstances when he has told me nothing about them?

"I have another suit," he admitted at last.

"Then please wear it on Saturday. And now you may go."

He looked at the ormolu clock. "It is not yet six."

"All the same, you may go. On other occasions perhaps I will give you letters to answer, but I do not wish to do that today. It is my birthday in a few days' time, and I shall be having a small dinner party. I need to make preparations."

I do not know what made me add that detail, but I am glad I did, for it restored good feeling between us. He smiled—he has a pleasant smile, when he chooses to use it—and said he hoped I would have a happy birthday.

Saturday, January 18th, late evening

Claude came to my birthday party, along with some of the chattering crowd. I had thought of inviting Diana, but she and Claude are like oil and water — or water and oil, I should say. She is water, he is oil. Anyway, they do not mix.

The evening was not a success, although Parkin and Henri had done their best. Parkin had lit all the lamps, set the dining table before my pair of long gilt-framed mirrors, and made the room gay. I had the gramophone playing as people arrived, and Henri produced several masterpieces of culinary art for our meal, but my guests were more interested in their own wit than in the music or the food.

I sat with my back to the mirrors, not wishing to view myself. There at the table, with my crutches behind me and my legs hidden, I was almost able to forget and believe myself charming. Then I would look up and see, through the dimly lit salon, the doors leading to the library. I was reminded of Vaughan with his shabby suit (he wore one that fit today, but it is far from new) and his straight posture that seems to judge my slouched shoulder, as his air of monkish virtue seems to judge my way of life. The memory irritated, like an insect bite that only gets worse when one scratches.

I had not invited Louis. Claude's man of the moment brought a friend intended for me, and after dinner the four of us went to the theatre. Claude set off first, while Parkin installed me in the carriage I inherited from my uncle, a Victoria with a handsome pair of black horses.

"I thought you would have a motor car," my escort grumbled.

"No, I do not like them"—while he plainly did, so we were off to a bad start.

I seldom go to the theatre these days. It is such a business to get there, especially on a frosty night, and there are so many stairs! Even if one's seats are on a level with the street, one must go up and down to reach them. Ours were in the middle of a row, some of the best in the house, but I had not thought how hot it would be, how cramped, and how awkward to find a place for the crutches.

I looked forward to the interval, but it gave me no relief. More stairs, and then we met two talkative young widows and their escorts, friends of Claude's. They recover remarkably well from their sorrow, these widows, but I suppose they have had a year or two to do it, and some husbands would be no great loss. No doubt there are other women still grieving, who do not flit to the theatre but lick their wounds behind closed shutters.

We were herded into a corner, and of course we had to stand the whole time. My shoulder ached from the pressure of the crutch. The heat and the lights made my head ache too, and I decided not to stay for the last act.

"My" young man (who is not mine and never will be) agreed to leave with me, although he did not seem pleased. The two of us went to Claude's rooms at the Ritz, where our supper was laid. Claude's servant brought us wine, but we could not eat until the others arrived, so we sat gazing at the table, failing to entertain each other.

Later it was not so bad—Claude's friend is a costume designer who had some intelligent things to say about the play—but I was not sorry when I could decently come home. I left the other fellow outside a café to seek diversions more to his taste, while I returned to the apartment alone.

I got off to sleep without trouble but woke in the night, as I often do after too much wine.

My leg throbbed. The infection is not gone as I had hoped. Lying in the darkness, I despaired of my future. Black dread flooded my mind when I thought of the weeks, months, and years rolling out endlessly ahead of me, nothing ever changing but my age.

I lit the lamp and took up this book to write, but it has done no good.

So my thirtieth birthday was a failure—as I am, as my life has been and always will be.

Just as my father warned me . . .

The day after my brother caught me in the summerhouse with a man I had foolishly invited home, my father summoned me to his library and asked, "What is your excuse for this unspeakable behaviour? Did the fellow somehow draw you in against your will?"

He was showing me a way out, but I had made up my mind through that long sleepless night that I would not hide my nature from him. "He was not to blame. Lust was the only culprit."

He paced back and forth in his library. "But why not go to a woman? I suppose you don't like streetwalkers . . . I can understand that. They are not always clean. But you could surely come to an arrangement with some reliable girl of the working class?"

"I have no interest in women."

He froze. "No interest? What do you mean? You are clearly not one of those . . ." He fluttered a hand to indicate an effeminate man.

"Perhaps not, but I belong with them. I have always been this way. It is a thing I cannot help."

My father frowned. "If you cannot overcome it yourself, you must consult a specialist. There are doctors, I believe, who treat such cases."

"I will not discuss it with a doctor."

"Then a clergyman?" He must have seen from my face what I thought of that. "You must do something, James! Men who give in to unnatural lust soon find it becomes a torture. It is the same with drink, or any vice. The more you indulge it, the more of a grip it will have on you, and the more miserable you will be. If you will not accept help, will you give me your word as a gentleman never to surrender to such an impulse again?"

I could not make a promise I knew I would not keep, so I didn't answer.

"You will not attempt to rid yourself of this perversion?"

Still I made no reply.

I had never seen his face so grim. He walked to the window as if he could not bear to look at me, his hands clasped behind his back. His voice was icy. "Then get you gone. You are no son of mine."

The memory is barbed wire, twisting in my gut.

The worst of it is that he was right. I did not believe, then, that my deepest desires could be a vice, but I cannot deny that the more I follow them, the unhappier I become.

I have grown to be a cynic, a cripple in every sense, twisted in mind, body, and spirit.

Why was I spared, when thousands of better men lie dead? Why do I live to do nothing but waste my time with men like that fellow tonight, who would spit in my face if I were poor?

How vile I am, how ugly and petty and futile. And I cannot change. It is too late. Perhaps it always was.

Men are still dying of their injuries, and I could join them. My revolver lies chill and heavy in its locked drawer. I can bring this downward spiral to a close, leaving before the curtain as I left the theatre, disappearing during an interval, inconveniencing no one.

Parkin, do not let this book fall into the hands of my family. My solicitor, Finlayson, has my will.

God have mercy on my soul.

6

Edmund's Journal
Sunday, January 19th, early hours

I am ill-tempered tonight and cannot sleep. I do not know why.

Colonel Clarynton objected to Charles's suit and wanted to buy me a new one, so I wore my own clothes yesterday. I cannot let him dress me, as if I were a servant in livery. In any case, I only wore Charles's suit to make sure he would not be attracted to me, and I need not have worried. If he prefers men, I am not the type he likes.

He stirs my pity at one moment, my anger the next. He has suffered so much and still suffers, but I wish he had learned to be civil.

He must know I do not welcome personal questions — I have made it clear — but he fires them at me all morning. "Do you have many friends in Paris?" or "What do you do in the evenings?" when anyone could see I cannot afford to have friends or to do anything in the evenings.

All I want is to be left alone to work in peace. Or is it? From the moment Parkin brought my lunch yesterday, I did not see my employer. I had all the peace and quiet I could have desired. And yet I was happiest in the morning, when I sat in the salon taking notes of all he said.

This book could turn out well if he applies himself to it. His mind is quick and incisive, and he knows his subject. He is still young and has the time and money to achieve something worthwhile. But he does not seem to take his work seriously.

He is the second son of an earl, Parkin tells me. The elder son went through the war in a government post and has established a family on the country estate, so they have no need of our colonel. I gather he was involved in some disgrace in England, although he has surely made up for that by earning the Victoria Cross. I wonder what kind of disgrace?

But here I am, doing what I dislike in him — speculating about his personal life.

Mama is wakeful too. I can hear her coming down from Robby's room, where she has been poking at the coals in the fireplace above mine. We keep his fire going all night in the cold weather, and I expect she has been up to make tea. I shall put down my pen and take some with her. She likes to hear about the colonel's apartment, about its plan and its furnishings. I can discuss those without becoming cross.

7

James's Journal
Sunday, January 19th, early hours

The gun was in its place, but the bullets were not. Parkin must have taken them away.

Shall I wake him and demand them?

I can imagine what he will say. *Well now, where did I put them? It's the middle of the night, sir. Won't you go back to bed while I look for them? Drink this – your pain medicine – it will help you sleep . . .*

He will not give them back. I shall have no bullets until I go out and buy more. Where is the nearest gunsmith?

But I will not do it. As soon as I pictured Parkin in the scene, I passed beyond the crisis. I can feel the despair ebbing away.

I was tempted to tear out the last page I wrote. It seems self-indulgent now, cowardly, the product of frustration and drink. I will leave it in, however, as a warning, to remind me of the depths to which I can sink.

Another dull day lies ahead, but I have the opening pages of my book to correct, and on Tuesday, Vaughan will come again. I believe he depends upon me for his survival, as do Parkin and my one-legged cook. I may be doing some good in this world, just by living.

So I shall stay in my seat at the theatre of life and watch whatever passes before my gaze until the final curtain falls.

Saturday, January 25th, morning

A week has gone by, and I have been out very little. The weather is grey and cold, with the wind whipping drizzle into one's face as soon as one steps onto the street. I have not written in this journal or done anything of significance except to spout words about chinoiserie and have my shoulder pulled and prodded. However, I am drinking less and sleeping better.

It is barely nine o'clock in the morning. I dressed early and breakfasted, and I cannot sit still in my chair. I am as restless as a fly beating against a windowpane. Vaughan comes at ten, and I am impatient for his arrival. I shall begin a new chapter today. I have not planned it thoroughly, but my mind is full of fine phrases.

I must note them down, or they may vanish into the ether before he arrives.

Evening

Diana came to tea. She is a real friend, and I might have told her a great deal, but I did not. I am afraid, I think, of what may emerge if I give anyone a glimpse of the box of writhing maggots that has taken the place of my soul.

She still has not chosen between her two suitors.

"You must decide," I said, "whether you wish to hold the reins or let your husband have them. It is not a question of who makes decisions on practical matters, but whose heart will be dependent on the other for its happiness. It is easier for men—at least, men of our class. We can involve money in the equation and keep control that way, even when we are at our most defenceless."

I feel defenceless with Vaughan. I want more of him than he is willing to give. I want every moment of his time and to know every thought in his head—but that is not what I am paying him for, and he grants me nothing outside his duties.

"You think it is easier to make it a commercial transaction?" Diana asked. "I suppose you are right, or so many men would not do it."

"But then marriage is a commercial transaction too, of a different kind."

"In some cases." She plucked at a loose thread on her tunic, and her expression grew serious. "I know what you mean about control, anyway. If I take Johnny, I must be careful not to let him hold the reins. He is younger than I am, and I could never relax. I should have to keep my looks and go on playing the game, always holding something back for fear of boring him. That is the choice—a man like Bill, who will be faithful but may bore me, or Johnny whom I may bore."

"You mean Bill who loves you, or Johnny whom you love?"

She laughed. "If you want to put it like that... you romantic."

Why do people marry? I once thought only women truly wanted that tie, and men did it because they fell in love and could not have the woman any other way. But many men support mistresses, yet even the wealthiest still marry. Is it for children, then—for the man to be sure a child is his, for the woman to know her children will be supported? Or are they seeking something more, something in the relation between the two people themselves, something almost spiritual? Does the unbreakable bond force one to plumb the depths of one's nature, and does that make it worthwhile?

Would I wish to marry, if I felt about women as other men do? Or—inconceivable—if men could marry men, would any of us do it?

Parkin and his butler, perhaps, but they are sixty.

"Are you not in love with either of them, then?" I asked.

Diana stood and walked to the window. "What is love? I am not sure I know. I thought I loved my husband when we married, but when he came back on leave he was like a stranger to me. We had only been apart a few months, and already the fire was gone to ashes."

"The war has killed true love," I said. "It has hardened our hearts—put a crust around them that nothing can pierce."

"Or perhaps it was always a pretence, and nobody was ever satisfied with one person for all their lives, not even Adam and Eve. Every couple thinks other couples are happy, but they are all putting on the same act."

"So we have no hope of finding anything that will last."

We stared at each other for a moment, both afraid, I think, that we had said more than we should, like children destroying each other's belief in fairies . . .

The soft tapping of the typewriter punctuated the silence like a distant drum. I thought at one time that the sound might annoy me, but it does not. It soothes, like raindrops falling on a roof when one is cosy and warm inside.

The tension flooded out of my shoulders.

Diana smoothed down her skirt and came to sit beside me. "May I not meet your secretary?"

"Of course. What an excellent idea." I rang for Parkin. "Ask Mr. Vaughan to come in, would you? And bring another cup, or tell him to bring his cup if he already has one."

Parkin went the long way round, out of the salon by the hall door. He never opens the doors between the library and the salon while Vaughan is here, except to show Vaughan into the salon after I have requested his presence. I suppose servants are trained in thousands of rules like this. How do they remember them all? I would not have made a good servant. And yet soldiers are like servants, doing what we are told without question.

Vaughan came in holding cup and saucer in one hand and papers in the other. If he was surprised to see someone with me, he did not show it.

I said, "Diana, this is —" I broke off there, but he did not speak. I had to add, "I do not know your Christian name, Vaughan."

It was a wonderful moment. I had the most natural reason to ask, and he could not, in all politeness, avoid telling me.

A hint of a frown darkened his brow, but he said simply, "Edmund."

Edmund! It is perfect. It fits him like the snuggest kid glove.

"Diana, this is Edmund Vaughan, my secretary. Vaughan, this is Lady Diana Grantleigh."

He bowed. "How do you do?"

"Do sit down," Diana said. "More tea?"

"No, thank you." He chose to sit at the table where he takes dictation, looking like a schoolboy taking tea with the headmaster's wife.

"Have you been in Paris long, Mr. Vaughan?" Diana asked.

He cleared his throat. "About six months."

"And how do you like it?"

"Very well."

"It is certainly the place to be just now — the centre of the world, one might say, with so many powerful men here, hammering out the details of the peace."

"Yes. If only they could have settled things that way in 1914," Vaughan — Edmund — said.

"Indeed." Diana turned to me. "I am told many of the delegates cannot understand each other, even when somebody translates. Their expectations conflict, and they are incapable of seeing the situation with other eyes. And they were all fighting on the same side! It will take six months to reach agreement."

"Longer," I said. "Meanwhile, the Ritz is unbearable, and we cannot enjoy Versailles without the company of a hundred pompous commissioners."

This flippant comment was designed to stir Edmund to earnest protest if he had strong feelings about war and peace, but he said nothing.

A moment passed, and then Diana asked, "Are you alone here, Mr. Vaughan?"

A muscle twitched in his cheek. "In Paris, you mean?"

"Yes."

He hesitated as if looking for a way out. Finally he said, "I am with my family."

Surely not a wife and children! He is so young, and besides . . . No, I could not imagine it.

Neither could Diana, apparently, for she said, "Your mother and father?"

"My mother."

His mother. I sat back—I had been on the edge of my seat. Yes, I could imagine a mother. And we had winkled out another secret!

I smiled at him. I could not help it. It might have been a wolfish smile, for he looked warily at me and then, with desperation, at the clock.

"It is getting late, Colonel Clarynton. If you would like me to finish today's pages before I go, I should perhaps . . ."

It was only a quarter past five, but I took pity on him and let him go. He crossed the room with every appearance of calm, but I am sure he was stirred up inside. He does not like to speak of his life outside these walls.

He might have believed I had asked Diana to quiz him. I wish I had thought of it—I could have given her a list of questions. She might not have consented, however. Her principles are unconventional, but she holds to them as if they were God's commandments.

Could I ask Claude to do it, or would Edmund evade his questions as he does mine? Etiquette would not require him to answer Claude. A titled lady has a power in conversation that no man of any rank can hope to possess.

The library doors closed behind him. "He seems very young," Diana said in a low voice.

"He is twenty-one."

"But he did not fight, did he, or drive an ambulance? He has seen nothing, I can tell. He is a babe in petticoats—in Paris with his mother! You must not corrupt him, James. It would be a sin."

"I am flattered that you think I could."

She stood and straightened her pearls in the mirror. "Oh, you could. I must go, but I warn you, if I find you have turned him into one of those men who is passed from hand to hand around your circle, I will never speak to you again."

How does she know so much? And how could she think I would allow that to happen to him? Edmund with another man—Edmund with Claude, for example ... no. The thought makes my stomach churn. When I picture it, I am rushing to them in my mind, grasping Edmund's arm and tearing him away.

Edmund with me ... I have imagined that, I admit. But in those dreams I have two legs and two eyes. I am the "handsome devil" I once was.

In waking life, an impassable gulf separates us. I am reminded of it with every painful move of my shattered limbs. Diana was right. He escaped the war—it has not touched him—while I am cut in pieces by it. Who would believe I am only eight or nine years older?

He will never see what I have seen. At least, I hope he will not.

When I look at him, I am reminded of what my life used to be. At his age, I was as innocent as he is. I saw the world spread before me like a vast banquet. But when I tasted it, every mouthful was poisoned.

The memories are bitter. I would rather forget that I was ever young and full of hope.

Had I thought of this before I engaged him, I might not have done it. And yet his presence does not weary me. It refreshes me—*he* refreshes me—as if it were better to remember than to forget.

I have been tempted to ask him to extend his duties one afternoon when Parkin is not here. I could offer him a small addition to his salary, and he might massage my shoulder or apply soothing ointment to my leg. And that might lead to more . . . not at once, perhaps, but the second time, or the third . . .

No, I must not do it. Some men are not affected by such transactions, but he would be. It would destroy the light in him. As Diana said, it would be a sin.

Besides, I am not sure he would consent. I fear the mere suggestion would drive him away forever, and I do not want to lose him. He is an excellent secretary, and he interests me when nothing else can.

And now I have begun to find out his secrets. It is delicious to be able to write *Edmund*.

So he is living in Paris with his mother? He is supporting her, I assume. Strange, when he could do that so much more easily in London.

8

Edmund's Journal
Sunday, January 26th

To church this morning. The choir sang like angels, moving me to tears. Did our choir at Finchley ever sound so divine? If so, I did not know it at the time, sitting in the stalls with my friends and enemies, passing notes and pinching each other when we thought the men in the row behind could not see us. Some boys used to warble rude words to the hymns. I cannot imagine the voices I heard this morning doing the same.

Robby would have a place in those choir stalls now, if he were not ill. He is still young enough, and his voice is pure, but he cannot hold a note without coughing. Mama does not sing hymns with him on Sundays but reads to him from the Bible or the Psalms and prays with him. She goes to church herself in the evening and on other days, heavily veiled.

I met Mme. H. on my way home, returning from her Roman mass. She chatted to me cordially as we walked. Her manner has changed completely now that she sees me going out to work three days a week.

But that is unfair. She is not a bad woman. She does not refuse to house Robby, as some landladies would. She even climbs to the attic to look in on him if Mama has to go out when I am working. Money matters more to her than it should, perhaps, but this house is all she has to support herself, her widowed daughter, and her little grandchild. She has to make it pay.

Last night I told Mama about Lady Diana Grantleigh, whom I met at the colonel's. I wish I had not mentioned her, for it has worried Mama. Lady Diana's people live near Akingbourne, and Mama used to know them—not Lady Diana herself, she is too young, but her father and grandparents.

Mama has told us many stories about the family. If Lady Diana had been introduced to me by her maiden name, I would have recognised it, and I would not have mentioned her visit at home. But she has been married and widowed, Mama said. Her wedding was in the society papers some years ago, and her husband died in action in the first year of the war.

Now that I know, I can see the effect of it. She looked barely older than me, but she had the same brittle tone to her voice that Colonel Clarynton has at times, a tone that warns one away from certain topics.

Mama asked if Lady Diana's father was also in Paris. I do not know, and I am reluctant to broach the subject with the colonel. Lady Diana's questions made me uneasy. She asked so many of them! I wondered for a moment if he had put her up to it, but I think not. They were questions that any lady might ask to open a conversation . . . but those are the most dangerous kind.

If she visits again while I am there, I shall plead illness and come home.

9

James's Journal
Tuesday, January 28th

They were here at half past nine to try the new leg. It is still not right. They insisted that I put it on, but either it does not fit or what remains of my own leg is not ready. In the end they removed it. I am still in pain from it now.

Vaughan came at ten, and I told him to go away. He went rather pale—I was abrupt, I suppose—but I was in no mood to be polite.

As he turned to leave, I said, "Wait a moment. I must have your address. There will be times like this when I need to rearrange your days. I could have sent a note and saved you the journey."

He froze like a frightened animal. "It is no trouble for me to come."

"Are you on the telephone?"

"No"—as I expected.

"Then what if I want you a day earlier, on Wednesday instead of Thursday, say? How should I let you know?"

He could not think how to answer that. I had cornered him. Unkind of me, no doubt, but wouldn't any employer expect to know his address?

I waited. At last he said, "You can send to thirty-eight Rue Michel-Ange."

"Thank you. Would you be so good as to write it down for me?" I did not want him to know it was engraved on my memory, never to be forgotten!

He wrote it, and I pocketed this treasure. Then he went away as instructed. I heard Parkin speaking to him in the hall, probably to explain my short temper. Without Parkin I should have no friends left.

Later I consulted a street plan. The Rue Michel-Ange is in Auteuil, leading away from the more fashionable part, near the southernmost tip of the Bois de Boulogne. Not the worst *quartier* in Paris, but far from the best.

I hope he does not wander in the Bois at night. Or do I mean I hope he does? It would imply he enjoyed certain experiences. I do not go there now, because my leg makes me vulnerable to thieves. But I have thought of it. If he were there —

What nonsense I write. Edmund would jump from the Eiffel Tower before he would offer himself in the Bois.

10

Edmund's Journal
Thursday, January 30th

We diverged from the usual plan this week. It has been unsettling, but I have seen the colonel in many different lights.

He had doctors there on Tuesday and ordered me away very brusquely. I was hurt, though I knew I should not be. His treatment must take first place.

He demanded an address where he could reach me in such circumstances. I wish he had not, but he was bound to ask for it sooner or later.

I thought he wanted me there yesterday, Wednesday, instead, but I must have misunderstood him. Parkin seemed surprised to see me and left me standing at the door while he "went to enquire." He came back after a moment. No, the colonel did not need me that day.

Not to be spoken to at all hurt more than being spoken to brusquely. I felt I had been treated like a hawker — turned away without the courtesy of an interview. Moreover, I had missed a day's work and must expect to be paid less this week. Perhaps he was tiring of the book. Would he terminate my employment? I passed an anxious twenty-four hours.

Today being Thursday, I went again. This time Parkin let me in but said the colonel was having a bad day and I must be as quiet as I could.

"Typing's all right. He likes the sound of that," Parkin told me. "Just go softly when you're walking around. I don't know what they did to him with that false leg, but it's set him right back. He's resting in the salon. He's left things for you to do in the library—some corrections, I think he said, and some letters to answer."

Relief flooded through me. His refusal to see me yesterday had not been related to the book or to me!

I went into the library and uncovered the typewriter. I retyped the corrected pages and turned to the letters. He had scrawled a note on each one to show how he wanted it answered, often just *yes* or *no* in a struggling, unsteady hand that stabbed me with pity.

I am beginning to know his style, so I was able to produce something for each piece of correspondence. When Parkin came in with my lunch, I had drafted answers to them all, ready for the colonel to sign. I told Parkin so.

"Then you may as well go home when you've eaten," he said. After a moment's hesitation, he added, "I didn't ought to ask, I know, but I wonder if you'd do me a good turn and take a note to a house in the boulevard? Do you pass that way?"

"Certainly."

I gave him paper and an envelope. As he began to write, he said, "It was my afternoon off, you see, and I was meeting a friend, but I won't go now. My friend wouldn't mind if he didn't hear from me—he'd guess what was up—

but if it isn't too much trouble for you to let him know, it'll save him hanging about."

Parkin has done so much for me that on an impulse I said, "Why don't you take your afternoon? I will stay with the colonel. I don't think I ought to go home just yet, anyway. He may feel better later and want to give me more work."

"Oh, I couldn't ask you to stay with him by yourself, Mr. Vaughan."

"Why not?"

"Well, there's personal things he wouldn't want you doing."

I guessed what he meant. Colonel Clarynton would never forgive me if I had to help him with a chamber pot. All the same, I said, "If you make sure he is comfortable before you go, he would be all right for an hour or two, wouldn't he? Then you could at least meet your friend and explain."

Parkin pursed his lips, then nodded. "I suppose I could do that, if I prop open the pantry door and this one, so you'll hear the bell if he rings."

He gave me instructions about the colonel's medicine. "One powder, no more, and not a minute before three o'clock, no matter how much he begs or shouts. He might threaten to dismiss you unless you'll let him have it early. Take no notice. He doesn't mean it. On the other hand, if he doesn't ask for a dose, don't give it. It's only for the pain. He takes it easiest mixed in a spoonful of honey. I'll put some on a tray for you."

"One powder in a spoonful of honey, and not until three o'clock. All right."

"And like I said, don't mind anything he might say. He's all drugged up and doesn't know who he's talking to half the time, so don't take it personal. And if he needs moving—like if he's got off the couch and needs lifting back up—don't try to do it by yourself. Ring down to the concierge, and he'll help you. He's used to it. The cook can't do it, with his leg, and anyway he's off now until five."

He was still giving me instructions as he put on his coat.

The apartment was utterly silent when Parkin had gone, except for the ticking of the library clock. I read over my work again and redrafted one letter. Then I turned to the bookshelves.

The colonel has many interesting books on art, philosophy, history... every subject. I could not settle to one, but glanced through several of them before climbing on a pair of steps to reach the upper shelves. Right under the ceiling I found a book with blank covers and took it down from curiosity.

I could not believe what I saw.

Inside were no words but only pictures—pictures of men unclothed. Sketches and engravings pasted onto the pages, and some photographs held in with corners, as in an album... one man alone or two clasped together, caressing each other, as in my dreams.

I know what goes on, of course, from the talk of boys at school and the sneers of the fellows at the bank. They always made it sound dirty and unpleasant. These pictures showed something beautiful. They showed love.

Desire overwhelmed me, making me tremble. My knees gave way, and I sat down with a thump on the top step, still clutching the book. How I wished to leap into the pictures and join those men! How I longed for them to open their arms to me and smile... I turned page after page, careful not to crease the thin interleaves, flushing with heat from my core to every extremity.

I have had a glimpse of another world, of heaven, and nothing will be the same again.

The feelings come back to me now as I write, still just as intense.

How will I look him in the eye? How will I sit typing day after day with the blank spine of that book mocking me—never daring to take it down for fear I will be discovered with it open in my hands?

There may be more albums like it. I did not finish looking at that one, because a noise came from the salon, a thud, as if he had dropped something.

I thrust the book back onto the shelf with shaking hands, climbed down, and went through to him, hoping he would not notice my discomfort.

He did not seem to see me at first. A chair had toppled over, but he lay motionless on the couch, staring straight ahead at a spot on the opposite wall.

His eye patch had slipped off. I had never seen him without it before. I had thought there would be a dressing underneath, but no—just the empty eye socket and the sunken skin around it.

He is so handsome! I can write it here, where nobody will decipher my shorthand. The handsomest man I have ever seen, with his dark brows, and his quick eye, and the mouth that twists and laughs so easily.

I noticed his looks on the first day, but they had never struck me with such force before. The patch is so big and black that when he is wearing it, one does not see much else. But there is nothing dreadful about the sightless socket beneath. It is a void, and the rest of the face gains from the contrast.

He lay on the couch in the exact pose of a man I had just seen in the book. I yearned to touch him. Of course he was clothed, but I could imagine sitting beside him. I might stroke his cheek . . . and so it would begin . . .

I could love his wounds. I could love his scars. I could love all of him.

I went nearer, intending to pick up the chair. He must have seen me then, or seen something—perhaps not me, because he said in a clear, sharp voice, "Tell those men not to show a light."

It shocked me out of my daydream. I straightened up and said, "Yes, sir!" as a soldier would. I thought it might mean he wanted the curtains closed, so I crossed the room towards them.

He called, "Parkin?"

I turned, and this time he seemed to be trying to focus on me. I went back to him. "It is Vaughan. Parkin is out. He will be back soon."

"Ah." He said something about a butler, then, "He is a happy man. I wish he could teach me the secret. I believe he tries."

I did not know what to say to that. He shifted on the couch, winced, and asked, "When can I have another dose?"

"In half an hour, Colonel."

He grunted and closed his eye. After a moment he said, "I wish you would not call me 'Colonel.' My name is James."

I took that to be one of the things he said but did not mean, of which Parkin had warned me. I cannot call my employer by his Christian name.

"Do you play the piano?" he asked.

"A little. Not very well. Shall I put on the gramophone?"

"No, play for me, if you please."

I went to the piano with great reluctance. Why had I admitted I played? I have no gifts in that direction. I had not touched a piano for several years, and in the meantime my fingers had become used to typewriter keys. Would they even remember the notes? Perhaps if I dawdled, he would forget about this and talk of something else. But no, he was watching me intently.

I flicked through his music and found a short piece by Mozart that was familiar. I put it on the stand and sat down. My shoulders were stiff, and my fingers hesitated on the keys. I attempted the opening bars, hit a wrong note, and began again.

"Edmund," he said, on the third beginning.

I stopped at once.

"Schumann said, 'When you play, never mind who is listening.' I do not care if you falter. It is only to take my mind off the pain."

So he knew I had been hoping to impress him. Ashamed, I started once more, and this time I did not stop. After a time I forgot myself, and the apartment, and even him, as if I had been back at home in Finchley with Mama's gentle voice correcting my playing, Robby resting upstairs, and Charles kicking a ball outside.

I could not find another piece I knew, so after the Mozart I played a simple tune from memory and sang to accompany it.

At the end of the song he gave a *harrumph* of satisfaction and relaxed back against the couch. "You sing better than you play. Will you sing again?"

So we passed the half hour. Then I gave him his medicine. He relaxed at the sight of it, and in the time it took me to take the tray back to the pantry, he fell asleep.

I hope he will have forgotten everything when I am next there. Then the memory of this afternoon will be mine alone to cherish.

11

James's Journal
Thursday, February 6th

Just as I seemed on the point of developing a delicious flirtation with my secretary, Loulou had to come and spoil it. My sins are catching up with me — karma, as they call it in the East. I am reaping what I have sown.

Edmund and I got on awfully well when I was laid low. I am less of a threat, I suppose, when immobilised by pain and delirium. He sang to me most sweetly. I asked him to call me James, and he did not do it, but I called him Edmund, and he did not object.

The next time he came, of course we went immediately back to "Vaughan" and "Colonel," which I am starting to dislike. I ought to have ended the war as I began it, a dashing young captain, but those of us still standing were promoted beyond any rank we deserved to fill the gaps left by the fallen.

Today, while I considered whether to make another move with Edmund or leave well alone — bearing in mind that I risk losing not only him but also Diana, one of my few living friends, if I pursue him — Loulou arrived uninvited.

It was the middle of the afternoon. He has never come so early before. Perhaps he hoped to catch me out in something.

His eyes darted around the salon, but there was nothing new to see. He came to my couch and kissed my cheek. "How are you, James?"

He took my hand and pressed it between his. His manner is so insincere! It has always been, I suppose, but for some reason it irritated me today. I drew back my hand and reached for the bell pull.

"It is early for tea, but I shall ask Parkin —"

"You English and your tea! I prefer coffee, no matter what time it is."

"Very well."

I ordered coffee for us both. We said little until it came. He went to the window and stood with his back to it, watching Parkin set down the tray.

When Parkin had gone, Loulou came nearer and said, "It has been so long, *chéri*. I have missed you."

How long had it been? Three weeks, perhaps? I had not seen him since my birthday. But no, it was not Loulou who came to the theatre with us that night, but a man whose name I do not recall. Longer, then — not since the beginning of the year.

Once I would have said, "I missed you too," whether I had or not, and everything would have gone on as usual. But as Loulou bent towards me, smiling, waiting for my reassurance, I saw a bubble of spittle on his lower lip, and in an instant he became a creature I could not bear.

So I said instead, "But you know, Louis, all things must end."

He jerked up and stepped back. His expression grew stormy, and he ran a hand through his hair. "Ah! It is that? As I thought. You have found someone else."

"No."

"No? Then do not speak of endings. I know you will wish to see me from time to time."

When I did not reply, he came to sit beside me on the couch and placed a hand on the thigh of my good leg. "Your Loulou is very fond of you, James."

The flesh is weak. My treacherous body stirred at his touch. Before this could become obvious, I took his wrist and moved his hand away.

Louis shook me off and turned his head towards the library. "What is that noise?"

The typewriter was going *tap-tap-tap* in the next room. I am so used to it that I had not noticed it start.

"It is my secretary. I am writing a book."

"Your secretary? *Tiens*! A man?"

I did not need to answer. We were speaking French, and I had used the masculine form. Louis jumped to his feet, crossed the salon, and flung open both of the double doors. I sat up to watch, apprehensive but amused at the idea of their meeting.

Edmund stopped typing, and they stared at one another. I could not see Louis's face, but I saw Edmund's. He held his head high and did not lower his gaze.

Louis let go of the doors, walked into the library, and prowled around the desk like a tiger. He bent towards the typewriter, where he took hold of the sheet of paper on the roller and pulled it out with one sharp tug. Retreating with his prize, he leaned against the wall to study it, brow furrowed and lips moving as he puzzled over the English words.

Edmund had made no attempt to stop him, which surprised me. I had thought he would defend his territory. Then I saw how he gripped his notebook, where my dictation was recorded in shorthand. The typing could be done again as long as he had those notes.

They made a striking contrast—Louis all flashing colour, Edmund pale as marble, but upright, tense, holding on to what mattered most.

Louis held out the sheet of paper. Edmund accepted it. Louis stared at him for a moment more, and Edmund met his gaze. Then Louis turned his back on Edmund and returned to me, closing the double doors. They had not spoken a word to each other.

After a moment, the typing started up again.

Louis sat down—not beside me on the couch, but in one of the Rococo chairs. "Well, it is not that one, it is evident. How English he is! You could not be interested in a creature so dull and plain and lacking in passion."

It is a long time since I thought Edmund plain, and I never thought him passionless. But I saw the trap and merely shrugged.

"Then your new friend may be the one you took to the theatre last month?" he asked.

So he had heard about that. "Perhaps there is no new friend. Perhaps I have other things to do with my time."

"You mean the book you are writing?" He glanced again at the library doors. "Jade is *jade*? The same word in English and in French? Like this?" He motioned to the green figure of a warrior on horseback on the lacquer table.

"Jade is *jade*, yes, but that is porcelain."

He picked up the ornament and examined it. "It is valuable?"

"Not really. It is a European imitation."

He set it down and turned back to me. "So you write a book about jade and porcelain. Good, it is an excellent occupation. But, James, you must not leave your Loulou friendless and alone."

He is nothing of the kind, of course, but he must have seen I was determined to have no more to do with him, and there is a certain game one has to play in these situations. He must pretend to be heartbroken; I must pretend to regret the circumstances that force me to stop seeing him. We both made the required moves as gracefully as one can.

It ended, as this game always does, with my writing one final cheque, many times bigger than usual, for him to fold into his pocket as he left.

And that, I trust, is the last I will see of Loulou.

12

Edmund's Journal
Thursday, February 6th

I discovered today that I was in error about my employer in one respect. I had thought that the gentleman at the Académie des Beaux-Arts—the one who first interviewed me, whom he calls Claude—was his *friend*. Not so. That must be a friendship of the ordinary kind. The other one, the *friend*, visited this afternoon and came into the library to inspect me.

He is a very different man, of a type for which I cannot have a great deal of respect, although he has a certain magnetic attraction. He is handsome, with thick black hair and flashing eyes, and—how can I describe him?—like a cat that stares from a high wall as one passes, and may do anything... purr, or hiss, or slash one's face with its claws.

He has "it," as they say. I envy him that. The colonel could not help but be caught.

He wore a blue silk waistcoat, the colour of the sky on a clear winter's day, and trousers exquisitely cut to show the firm limbs beneath.

Does he go to Colonel Clarynton's tailor, I wonder? Would I have been dressed like that if I had accepted the colonel's offer? Or does he have his own tailor, like Parkin?

And who pays?

13

James's Journal
Tuesday, February 11th

I am determined to know more about my secretary. He is quiet and self-contained on the surface, but I sense some great turbulence below.

Today I faltered a little as I was crossing the salon. He noticed—he notices everything—and said, "May I carry those papers for you?"

I was annoyed at my weakness, but I said, "Thank you," and let him take them. In the process, I let go of one of my crutches and wrenched my shoulder catching it. Flustered and humiliated, I swayed and lost my balance.

He gripped my arm. "Let me help you sit down."

To need help to sit down! This was too much. "No!" I cried, pushing him away. It was madness, but I could not bear to be dependent on him.

So I staggered again and fell. Then I had no choice—I had to let him help me up, because I could not reach the bell. Had I been alone, I would have shouted for Parkin, but it would have been absurd to shout when Edmund was there.

He is stronger than he looks. His hands are firm and sure. I warmed to his touch, but at the same time I resented his capability.

I thought of what I had said to Diana, that we must control or be controlled. He was controlling me, not only with his hands but with his very nature. He has a power over me that I do not like but cannot govern. He arouses in me an insane desire to seize him in my arms, tear off his dark glasses, and gaze into his eyes — to kiss his beautiful mouth — to bind him to me forever and make him mine — mine and mine alone.

What nonsense I am writing! It is only because I am so helpless, and because I cannot have him, that I feel so strongly — wanting him more than I ever wanted any man . . .

I made another misstep as I regained my balance on the crutches, and for a moment the pain in my shoulder was so great that I was conscious of nothing else. I reached the couch with Edmund's help, and things went black. Then I heard Edmund's voice saying, "Take a sip of brandy, please."

He sounded — could it be anxious? He did not seem to have called Parkin, or perhaps Parkin was out. In any case, Edmund was ministering to me himself.

I sipped. Then, with the pain fading to a dull throb, I saw what a fool I had been.

"Forgive me," I said. "I am not always polite when offered assistance. The aim of convalescence, it seems to me, is to become more independent, so when people offer to help me I imagine they wish to hinder my recovery."

He smiled. "That was not my intention."

"I realise that. I say it because you seem to understand my situation very well."

He nodded but moved away from me to sit at the table where he takes dictation.

"Perhaps you have a near relation wounded in the war?" I asked. This could be a reason for his being so long in Paris with his mother — if a father or brother lies in hospital here, still hovering on the brink of life or death, too ill to be transported home.

But he said simply, "No," and turned a page in his notebook. "Do you want to look over the beginning of chapter four again?"

I took another sip of brandy and set down the glass. "As you like. Read it to me, if you think it will help me see where to go next."

His voice was emotionless as he read. All the disturbance of the last few minutes appeared to have affected me alone. I made an effort to put aside my heated feelings and listen.

I had come to a dead end in the story of chinoiserie. Chapter four did not show me the way out, so I asked him to summarise each page of the first three chapters. His quiet voice calmed me, but when I paid attention to the words — my words — they seemed utter rot.

I would have given up the whole project then and there, had I employed any other secretary. But I did not want to let Edmund go.

"What do you think of it?" I asked him.

"I?" He swallowed. I had never put that question to him before.

"Yes, you. You must have some opinion."

"I do not know anything about the subject."

"You did not, perhaps, when we started, but you should know a little now. Have these chapters failed completely? Have they taught you nothing?"

"No, I have learned something about the development of this form of art, but not—"

He seemed unable to go on.

"Not what?"

He glanced at the door as if he wished to escape this conversation. But this was not a personal question. It was directly related to his employment. He could not evade it, and clearly he does not like to lie. His own honesty forced him to answer.

"I have not learned why it matters—why anybody should care, if they do not already appreciate this form."

"The book is too technical?"

"No, I see that it is intended for the general reader . . . if you mean to publish it."

His last words went into me like a dagger, bursting the bubble of illusion I had built up around the "work" for which I had engaged him. I leaned back and gave a bitter laugh.

He had understood too well. He saw that it did not matter whether the book was ever published, that it was only something to occupy my time, that I was not serious, that I was paying him for his presence, not for his typing, because the words he typed had no importance.

In that moment I saw my life for what it was, as I had on the night of my birthday—a desolate and worthless thing. Nothing I did had any significance. Nobody came because they wanted to see me. Some were here because I paid them; others came to enjoy fine dinners and each other's company in comfortable surroundings. The ones I considered true friends, Diana and Claude, visited because they were sorry for me. They humoured me, pandered to me, and talked about love as if it could still have a part in my life—as if I were not as unlikely to inspire it as a toothless old man of ninety. I was an object of pity, even to my paid secretary.

Edmund must have seen some of this in my face, for he leaped from his chair. "No, you have misunderstood me! I do not mean the book is bad."

I did not want to hear flattery, not then. I waved him away. "You have not told me anything I did not already know. Let us say there is room for improvement."

"It only requires a little rearrangement—an expansion of some of the ideas. May I tell you exactly what I think?"

"Tell me whatever you like."

I felt numb. I no longer cared what was in his mind. I laid my head on the soft silk of the cushion and closed my eye, wishing only to sleep forever.

The book had lost all interest for me. It was foolish, nonessential, like chinoiserie itself, existing only to give an aimless person something on which to fritter his time and money. The whole of life is like that, I thought—a thing without purpose, our only aim being to pass the time between birth and death as pleasantly as possible and avoid pain. But pain is unavoidable, so what is the good of anything? Why live at all?

The bullets—I must get some today...

Edmund drew his chair closer. I heard it slither over the rug. I imagined I knew what was coming. He had to reawaken my interest in the work or lose his job, so he would now become like Loulou, trying to win me over with soothing words in a velvet voice. They all had their ways to get what they wanted from me. What a fool I was, not to have seen it before.

When he spoke, however, his voice was as impersonal as always.

"You should be more committed to it. You do not take it seriously enough. A writer—as I understand it—naturally has moments when his work seems to sparkle with brilliance and moments when it seems hopelessly dull. If you give up at the low times, you will never finish, but if you persevere, in the end you will find you have produced something of value. It is always worth seeing things through and doing the best we can, is it not? That is the only way to get satisfaction from our lives... or so it appears to me."

I opened my eye. He was close beside me, but I felt nothing, only a desire to have done with it all. I was the emperor with no clothes, seeing at last what everyone else must have seen ever since I was injured, that I had been written out of the play of life, and the fabric of my days was all pretence.

"It is good of you to take an interest," I said politely.

He bit his lip. "It is only my impression, of course, but it seems to me you know a great deal about the subject, and it is coming out too fast. You have told the beginner too much too soon, without showing why this form of art fascinates you. If you would take it more slowly and consider what each piece means to you, I believe you could transmit your appreciation to the reader, and then you would not have these structural problems. You have plenty of material."

I raised my head a little. "You mean I have condensed it too far?"

"Yes. At least, I think so." He went on talking, coming out of his shell to show real understanding of my work and even admiration, as if my misery called this forth in him when my self-assurance had not. He spoke intelligently of each chapter, of each paragraph.

He was not only trying to cheer me up, I realised. The book must have meant something to him, or he would not remember it well enough to dissect it point by point. He had been truthful when he said he thought it worthwhile. He believed I could do this and do it well, if I made more effort to overcome my self-pity.

He did not say this in so many words, but it was in every sentence, in his manner of speaking. He grew animated, and at one moment he was so carried away that he took off his dark glasses and waved them in the air for emphasis.

My heart gave a bound. His eyes are beautiful! — a deep blue-green, like the sea on a perfect summer's day, framed by the longest and thickest lashes I have ever seen. I felt a strange mixture of awe and excitement, as if a curtain had been drawn back to show me a future full of happiness beyond anything I had imagined.

He must have seen this in my expression, for he stopped in midsentence. A flush came to his cheeks, and he put the glasses back on.

I think he wears them only to hide his eyes from me, and now I see why! I would not dictate a word if I could gaze into those eyes instead.

He went on speaking, with more restraint, but he had made his point. I interrupted him.

"I see what you mean. I will begin again and consider the significance of each item. Perhaps we could sketch out a plan?"

He took up his notebook and pen, and we devised a new structure for the book.

It will be a lot of work, and it will not always interest me, but I must put up with that. I was expecting too much of it. I cannot make it my whole purpose in life, or I shall fall into despair when it goes badly, as it sometimes will. Nor must I reduce it to being only an excuse to spend time with my secretary.

He can help me, perhaps, more than I have let him do until now—not by telling me what to write, but by telling me what not to write. Beyond that, I do not know what our relation might be. I cannot control it. I do not hold the reins.

Thursday, February 13th

He came again today. I now live for Tuesdays, Thursdays, and Saturdays, and I swing from joy to tedium—an uncomfortable state, but an improvement over unremitting tedium.

Today began well. In his absence yesterday, I had put flesh on the bones of the plan we had drawn up. He made a typed version, helping me to assign things to their right places.

"I am pleased you know nothing about chinoiserie," I said, as we assembled the notes for a chapter on wallpaper. "If you did, I think you would write a better book than mine."

Before he could deny this, Parkin came in and cleared his throat. "Luncheon is served."

"Oh—but we are in the middle of an important discussion. Can it not wait?"

"It is a soufflé, sir."

"Then we must eat it together. Lay another place in the dining room, Parkin. Mr. Vaughan will lunch with me today."

Parkin sniffed. "Very good, Colonel."

The sniff and the use of *Colonel* instead of *sir* meant he disapproved. I did not see why. Edmund must have sensed something, for he turned to Parkin with a furrowed brow, as if for guidance.

To forestall any objection, I said, "It is only this once, and you may take your usual hour afterwards, Vaughan."

Neither of them spoke. I led the way to the dining room, victorious.

"Won't you take off your glasses?" I suggested as we sat down.

"No, thank you. I can see very well with them on."

Ha! He did not claim to need them, only that they did not prevent him seeing. They are a prop and nothing else, I am sure of it.

We ate the salad, and then Parkin brought in the soufflés—two of them, prepared for our separate lunches. He served Edmund first, treating him as my guest. Was that correct? It may have been a subtle message of Parkin's. If so, it was too subtle for me.

I was afraid he would hover, so when we were served, I said, "That will be all for now, thank you, Parkin." The *thank you* slipped out as a sop to him, a sign of how nervous I was. It was a mistake. It is one thing to lose the reins to Edmund, but if I let Parkin get them, I shall be wrecked on the rocks of good manners.

Edmund's head was down, his gaze apparently trained on his plate. However, tension had appeared in his shoulders. His eyes might have told a story, if I could have seen them.

Perhaps a compliment would put him at his ease, I thought. "You answer my letters so well that I have suspected you of reading my mind. I should be glad if you would help me by suggesting improvements to the way I phrase things in the book when you think of them."

"Certainly." He spoke without hesitation, but his manner was distant. I have not seen another spark of the enthusiasm he showed on Tuesday.

"Do you ever write?" I asked. "Your own letters, of course, but anything else?"

"Sometimes."

"What sort of things?"

Was he an embryo novelist, I wondered, struggling to complete his first work? Was this why he had come to Paris? No. Novel-writing is not like painting. One does not need a teacher, and people seem able to do it anywhere.

He had not answered. I put down my fork to show him I was waiting for his reply and would not let him escape. I guessed he would not lie, so if I got anything out of him at all, it would be the truth.

"I write a journal," he admitted.

"Oh! I should like to see it."

The words slipped out in my delight. At once I saw they were not well chosen. No doubt I appear in his journal, and not always in a flattering light.

"I mean, to know its structure and so on," I added with haste. "I keep a journal too."

"I believe many people do."

I would not let him divert the subject to "many people." I had found common ground between us and did not intend to be moved from it.

"Yes, we do it because we are lonely, I think. We need some form of expression when we have no one with whom to unburden our hearts. Wouldn't you agree?"

"I suppose so."

"You are lonely?"

He took a piece of bread, buttered it, and set it on his side plate without taking a bite. "Isn't everyone, from time to time? Regarding your first draft, Colonel Clarynton, I could separate the pages so they can form the basis of a larger number of new chapters."

"I would rather start afresh, with no reference to them."

"Very well, but I will keep them in case you wish to use them as a prompt at any time."

He had successfully deflected me from personal matters again. Then Parkin came in on some excuse or other, and I could not get back to the subject.

After our lunch, Edmund took his customary hour. It was raining, so he did not go out. I wonder what he does on those days? Does he sit in the library writing his impressions of me in his journal? No, he would not risk it here. He brings a book to read, I expect.

The hour seemed long to me, with nothing to do but wait for him to return to his duties. Parkin is right. It is better for us not to have lunch together. Alone I eat slowly, look at the newspapers over coffee, and pass most of the hour that way, but if I eat with Edmund, I have to let him go until well into the afternoon.

Today it was almost half past two when we resumed work. We had barely finished constructing a plan for the new book when Parkin came in with the afternoon post.

"You may leave it on the table," I said. "Or — No, bring it to me, please. I will open it, Vaughan, and see if there is anything you can answer. My eye is growing tired, and I will soon need to stop work for today."

Edmund frowned and leaned forward as if concerned for me, so I added, "They tell me I may have a new eye in a month or two. Glass, of course, so it will not take the strain from the other, but I shall feel very different without this patch."

"I am happy to hear that."

With these words he bestowed one of his rare smiles upon me. A thrill of pleasure crept over me, warming me inch by inch. I said no more, not wishing to spoil the moment, but turned my attention to the post.

There was something in Diana's hand and a fatter missive from Aunt Adelaide, my father's sister, who enjoys disobeying him by maintaining an occasional correspondence with me. I put them to one side and opened the business letters first, passing them to Edmund one by one with instructions he barely needed. I slit the last envelope and unfolded the sheet inside.

"A bill from Malendon & Cie. Did we not pay that?"

"I do not recall it," Edmund said.

"Would you be so good as to fetch the chequebook?"

He went to the library. He was some time, and he came back with empty hands.

"Not there?" I asked.

"I cannot see it."

"Try the bureau in this room."

I gave him my keys. He searched the drawers and returned to his seat, shaking his head.

"I do not know where I have put it, then." I rang the bell. "Parkin, do you have the household chequebook for any reason?"

"No, sir."

"Well, will you see if it is in the bedroom?"

Parkin came back with a chequebook, and I waved him towards Edmund. "Go through the stubs, will you, Vaughan, for a payment to Malendon? It would have been towards the end of January, I think."

Edmund took the book from Parkin with a smile of thanks (he has plenty of smiles for my servant), and Parkin left the room. I read Diana's note, inviting me to a party where she promises I shall meet both Bill and Johnny. I put that aside and glanced over my aunt's letter. It was ten pages long, but the only real news was the death of a family dog.

Then I became aware of a certain stillness in Edmund. I looked up. His face was pink, and he did not seem to be breathing.

"What is it?" I asked sharply.

He cleared his throat. "I think Parkin must have brought the wrong chequebook."

I took it from his hands and flipped open the cover. The book was almost a new one, and I had written *Louis* on every stub. The sums, of course, were large.

I spoke as calmly as I could. "This is over, you know."

"There is no need to explain, Colonel Clarynton."

Something in his voice stabbed at my heart. I should almost have said he sounded hurt, but that cannot be possible. Was he embarrassed? Repelled by my perversion? I wish I could have seen his eyes, but the glasses hid them.

He collected his papers and stood. "I had better answer these letters."

I let him go. Any protest would only have made things worse. He typed my correspondence, brought it to me to sign, and left to post the letters on his way home.

I found the household chequebook later, in the dining room. We had not paid Malendon, but I did it myself this evening. I do not want to raise the matter with Edmund again.

He has seen my payments to Loulou. Damn, damn, damn.

14

Edmund's Journal
Friday, February 14th

Mama noticed I was quiet last night while she mended Robby's shirt in the lamplight, by the fire. It soothes me to be with her while she works. She does everything so calmly.

"What is the matter, Edmund?" she asked. "Something has troubled you today."

I did not know how to answer.

"You can apply for other posts if this one does not suit you," she added. "It is easier to get one when you have one, as with so many things in life."

I watched her needle pass in and out of the seam until it stopped and she looked up at me. Then I said, "The work suits me very well. The book is taking shape, as I told you. But the colonel's questions unsettle me, and now I have found . . . a weakness in him, a weakness of character."

"And you are disillusioned? You seemed to admire him a great deal at first."

"I did. I still do. He has a quick mind and such courage! He must often be in pain, but he rarely mentions it. He never blames others for his suffering . . . never curses the Germans or the war-mongering government or—"

I broke off, thinking of Charles.

She put down her sewing. "So you're disappointed to find he has a fault? Can you not guess what I will say?"

I smiled and sighed at the same time. "You will say that nobody is perfect."

"Yes. It's good that you see his weaknesses. We all have them, but we are often blind to them in those we admire, and then we are so easily misled."

I suppose she had my father in mind, but she did not say so, and I did not ask. Mama and I talk so often and agree on so many things that an outsider might think we have complete confidence in each other. But we skirt around our painful past with veiled hints, never tackling anything outright.

"He is not happy." I meant the colonel, and I meant it to excuse his paying that young man to be his companion. No, let me say it—his lover.

But why do I need to find excuses for him? Why shouldn't he enter into an arrangement like that if he wants to and the man is willing? It is not a criminal offence here in France and has not been since the revolution.

His relations with that man are not my business. Besides, he told me the affair is over.

I do not mind his preference for men, only that he pays them. Yet why should it affect me? It offends the romantic in me, perhaps. But his life has been torn apart, with little room for romance. Is it fair to call his transactions a weakness? Have I the right to judge?

I am all churned up inside—even now, a day later. My feelings are so changeable, I hardly know what they are. I wish I could have told Mama exactly what had happened, but how can one speak of these things to a lady?

As he said, I have no one to whom I can unburden my heart . . . only this journal.

The weather has turned cold and dry again. It is good for Robby. The doctor came this morning and said fresh air would benefit him now. He may walk from time to time in the Bois, if he goes slowly and has someone with him who will make sure he does not overtire himself.

So I have promised Robby an excursion on Sunday, weather permitting. He was excited and asked what we will see. People taking their promenade, I said — on foot, in carriages, or on horseback, depending upon their station in life. There is little else at this time of year. But people interest him more than anything, so he is happy.

Later

I have just collected a note in the colonel's hand, on this significant date! My heart has never beaten so fast — with hope or fear, I do not know.

But of course it was not a valentine. He writes to tell me he has accepted an invitation to visit a country house decorated in the chinoiserie style. He leaves early tomorrow morning and will be gone for a week.

I am to continue to go to work on the usual days. The concierge will let me into the apartment, and my employer will communicate with me by post.

It will be strange not to have him there, but after my embarrassment over the chequebook, it will also be something of a relief. Parkin is going with him, and the colonel has given the cook the week off, so I shall be alone with The Book . . .

I do not mean the book he is writing.

15

James's Journal
Château de Rignelle, Monday, February 17th

It irks me that Edmund knows I must pay for my pleasures. I did not mind his meeting Loulou when Loulou's attentions appeared to flatter me, but now that Edmund knows his true motive in visiting me, the memory of their encounter is not so amusing.

Anyone looking at me could guess it, perhaps — anyone who knew the world — but guessing is not the same as knowing. Worse, Edmund has seen how high are the sums I must pay.

I am furious with Parkin. I suspect he brought my personal chequebook on purpose, to warn Edmund against me. He must have thought Edmund's virtue was at risk because we ate lunch together. How absurd!

Parkin denied it, of course — or rather, he put on a grave expression and made maddening half denials, such as, "I am sorry you think me capable of it, sir." But if he had admitted it, I would probably have dismissed him on the spot, so perhaps it is fortunate he did not.

I knew I would not be able to face Edmund on Saturday, so I reminded the Countess of Rignelle that she had extended me a permanent invitation to visit the family pile, which escaped the revolution and any subsequent redecoration and is an example of chinoiserie applied almost to excess. Indeed, many people would argue that I should strike *almost* from that sentence.

The family is not in residence, except for one elderly aunt whom I encounter across the table at every meal. I spend my days taking notes and making sketches, and then I send it all to Edmund with instructions to make what he can of it. Parkin spends his time, I hope, reflecting upon his crime and his punishment, *viz* being separated from his butler for a week.

So here we are, buried in the countryside at the worst time of year, when all around is bleak. In summer, it might be pretty here.

As I wrote that, my mind was flooded with a vision of myself and Edmund in a house like this in June, with Edmund not my secretary but my own man, staying with me by his free choice. I would sit at the piano and play while he sang, and we would dine on the terrace by candlelight and make love as the moon rose . . .

I clutch at my pen. It cannot be. I am a half-blind cripple, with wounds of mind and body that will never heal, wounds I never want him to see. Had it not been for the war, I might have had it all — sunlight and music and his laughing eyes. Instead, those eyes are hidden from me, guarded behind glass like the precious jewels they are.

Château de Rignelle, Friday, February 21st

I have a few minutes to write before the carriage comes to take us to the station. We are going back to Paris earlier than I had planned.

When the midmorning post arrived, I opened Edmund's note first, as I always do. His letters are never more than half a page, concerned only with business, but it cheers me to see his signature and know he is there in my apartment taking care of things for me.

Today, however, his message made me groan.

>Dear Colonel Clarynton,
>I enclose the typescript of your notes dated the 18th inst., divided according to your chapter headings. Is the detail of a peacock from a wallpaper or a plate?
>Mr. Duquesne called and asked for your address in the country. You had not authorised me to give it out, so I did not. I told him I would forward any letter he cared to write, but he did not leave anything with me.
>Yours sincerely,
>E. Vaughan

"Did you say something, sir?" Parkin asked.

I put the letter down. "Louis has been there."

"*Bothering Mr. Vaughan?*" Parkin sounded as shocked as if I had said Louis had been charged with murder. More shocked, possibly. Bothering Mr. Vaughan may be a greater crime in his eyes.

"He must have got past Antoine. I hope he did not make a scene—Louis, I mean—but I am rather afraid he will have. Damn. What will Vaughan think of me? I thought I had made it clear to Louis that he has had all he will get. I shall have to speak to him again."

"Begging your pardon, sir, but couldn't you ask a lawyer to do it? It's the best way to deal with that class of person, from what I've seen."

I nodded. Parkin saw a great deal, I imagine, in forty years of confidential service to a duke.

"I do not like to think of Mr. Vaughan being insulted, Parkin. Will you try to find out what went on, when we get back? I know he will not tell me."

"Yes, sir. I can ask Antoine, if Mr. Vaughan doesn't wish to speak of it."

"A capital idea." I reread the letter. "It may not have been too bad. He has not resigned."

"I don't believe he can afford to resign, whatever happens," Parkin said darkly.

He is probably right. In any case, Edmund should not be a target for people whose dispute is with me. I folded the letter back into its envelope, slipped it between the pages of my notes, and went to the window. The gardens were clothed in a damp grey mist.

"This is ugly country," I said. "No wonder they wanted to brighten the place up inside. Pack for me, would you? I have done all I need to do here, and it is time we went home."

"Certainly, sir."

Parkin had a spring in his step as he left the room. Back to Paris—back to his butler—back to Edmund. If it were possible to spring on crutches, I believe I would be springing too.

16

Edmund's Journal
Friday, February 21st

For the most part I have enjoyed my days alone in the colonel's apartment, although it is very quiet without him. No bells—no clatter from the kitchen—no tuneful humming coming through the double doors. He loves music but cannot play because of his shoulder, so in his more cheerful moods he hums. I hardly noticed the sound when he was here, but I miss it now he is away.

Antoine, the concierge, unlocks the apartment and hands me the post as I arrive each morning. There is always at least one packet of work for me from the colonel. I walk softly to the library, as I did when he was ill, so as not to disturb the atmosphere. Then I settle at the typewriter. His letters I forward, unless I see from the return addresses that they are tradesmen's bills or catalogues, which can await his return.

Antoine's wife brings me coffee, because Henri is not here. The colonel must have arranged this for me—or perhaps it was Parkin. It was kind of one of them, in any case. At half past twelve I go out to buy bread for my lunch and eat it with cheese from the pantry, and I make my own tea with bread and jam at the usual time. Sometimes more work arrives by the afternoon post, but I stay until six even if I have nothing to do.

Looking at "the book of masculine delight" is not good for me — it only increases my feverish dreams — but I cannot resist taking it down from the top shelf when my work is done.

Until yesterday, the only noise was a pedlar crying his wares in the street or the ringing of the telephone, which always makes me jump. The colonel told me not to answer it so I do not, though sometimes its strident bell goes on and on, echoing through the apartment like a bird in pain.

Yesterday I had a visitor. He did not knock or announce himself. I was typing, and when I paused to roll in a new sheet, I heard footsteps in the salon.

I knew at once that it was not Antoine. This was a light step, and Antoine is a heavy man. A burglar? I froze, unable to move, as the steps passed from the salon to the corridor, going towards the bedrooms.

I thought of the telephone. I could call the police. The instrument is in the hall, near Parkin's quarters, so I crept across the salon to the dining room, avoiding the corridor, and put my head carefully around the door. I saw nobody, so I went out — but just as I reached the little table where the telephone sits, the visitor emerged from the colonel's bedroom. It was the young man in the blue silk waistcoat, whose name I now know is Louis Duquesne.

We stared at each other for a moment, and then he said, "Where is he?"

"He is not here. He has gone out of Paris."

"Where? To Versailles?" He came closer. His hair was unkempt, and he looked less well cared for than when I had seen him before. However, his hands were empty, so I did not think he was there to steal.

"No, he has gone to a château in the country for his research."

"With whom?"

"With his servant, Mr. Parkin."

His eyes flashed, and he laughed. "With his servant! Bah—that is not what I meant, as you know very well. We are the same, you and I, and you are not stupid. If he is gone to the country, he will not take only an old servant."

Heat rose to my cheeks. I *am* stupid. I had not considered he might have gone with a *friend*. It is possible. How would I know? But if he has, the man cannot be taking much of his time, or I would not receive such thick packets of work.

"Give me the address," Duquesne said. "I will go and see."

He spoke as if he assumed I would unite with him against this imaginary rival, but I had no desire to help him. My duty is to the colonel, whether he has a new *friend* or not.

"I cannot do that. If you want to write a note for him, I will send it."

Duquesne pursed his lips and looked me up and down. "You are very loyal. But you are wasting yourself, and it is a pity. One does not remain young forever. You have handsome eyes"—I have been working without the dark glasses while the colonel is away—"and you could earn a lot more than your pitiful salary if you fed yourself better and made a little effort with your clothes. His heart is mine, but men need variety. Or, if you prefer, I could introduce you to—"

He did not say to whom he could introduce me because Antoine arrived at that moment, panting from the climb, with a face like thunder.

Duquesne turned to him. "Do not trouble yourself, *monsieur le concierge*. I am leaving." He stalked to the door and went through it without looking back.

Antoine lifted his foot as if to kick him down the stairs, but of course he did not do it. Instead he hurried to me, cursing in French. "He slipped past my wife. It is lucky she told me. You do not seem well. Was he violent?"

My heart was racing and my teeth were clenched—Duquesne's words had stung—but I forced myself to take a deep breath and speak calmly.

"No, I am not hurt. What is his name? I must let Colonel Clarynton know he was here."

He spelled the name for me and added, "You should bolt the door when you are here alone."

I lay awake last night, thinking of everything Duquesne had said. A confusion of feelings has gripped me and will not let go. Anger, that he could insult me so; shame, because he is right, we are alike; jealousy, for what he has had with the colonel and may have again; and pain, because the colonel may not have told me the truth when he said the affair was over.

17

James's Journal
Paris, Sunday, February 23rd

Edmund did not seem surprised to see me when he entered the apartment yesterday. He must have heard downstairs that we had returned. Antoine had already muttered to Parkin about Loulou's visit, for which I am sure they blame me. Unfortunately, Antoine only arrived in the apartment as Louis was leaving, so he does not know what passed between him and Edmund.

I talked a little about our journey while Edmund settled at his dictation table. Then I said, "I am sorry about the interruption you suffered the last time you were here."

He opened his notebook to a fresh page. "You do not need to apologise. Your friends may visit, of course."

"Louis has a hot temper. Perhaps he raged at you, when he found me not here?"

"Not at all. Here is your sketch of the peacock design. As I told you in my letter, I did not know whether to class it with the wallpapers or the china."

It was useless. He will not discuss anything but work—not my life, not his own.

Now it is Sunday, and I must pass all of today and tomorrow before he comes again. The hours stretch ahead of me like a parched desert. His work from yesterday is corrected, and it is only noon. I do not need to rest. I have been better lately and want to do more. Tomorrow I shall go to hear an opera singer at a gathering hosted by the Italian delegation. This afternoon? I believe I shall drive in the Bois de Boulogne...

Later

A fortunate excursion! I have seen him and uncovered another secret!

It was not pure chance. I chose the Bois knowing he lived nearby, and I watched for him. In fact, I gave so much attention to the people on foot that I was late in acknowledging several ladies of my acquaintance in their carriages, including the Countess de Rignelle, who directed a cold stare at me through her lorgnette. Even so, I almost missed him because I expected to see him alone or with his mother, and instead he was with a boy, ten or eleven years old.

Edmund's head was bent as he talked to the child, his hat obscuring his face, but my heart knew his posture and thudded against my ribs. I made the groom turn at the first opportunity, and we went back.

The boy's eyes were on the horses as we slowed alongside. Edmund glanced up—he was not wearing the glasses—and stiffened. He tipped his hat and drew the boy closer to him. Whether he was protecting the boy or hoping the boy would protect him from me, I could not tell.

Fate was on my side for once. The weather had changed quickly, and the fine day had turned damp. I leaned out of the carriage.

"Good afternoon, Vaughan. I fear it is beginning to rain. May I take you home?"

Edmund looked up at the sky. "It is only a shower."

The boy shivered in his thin coat. I spoke in the sharp tone I use when I want to hide my real motives from Edmund. "The child is cold, and you are a long way from the gates. You will be home much faster if you swallow your pride and accept."

Edmund flinched, and the two of them exchanged a glance I could not read. Then Edmund said, "Very well. Thank you. This is my brother, Robert. Robby, this is my employer, Colonel Clarynton. I will hand him up, sir."

His brother! I had never heard of a brother before—and Edmund never calls me *sir*. He did it then, perhaps, to show the boy how to address me, but I did not wish to converse with his brother.

I said, "There is only room for two with my crutches, but he will enjoy riding with the groom. I remember what a treat I thought that was, as a child."

The boy moved eagerly towards the man on his high seat, but Edmund said, "No, you are right—he is cold and needs the shelter of the hood. I will sit with the driver."

Before I could think of an objection, he whispered something to the boy and helped him onto the step. Edmund climbed up to the front seat, so all I saw of him was the back of his shabby coat and hat. I was not pleased, but I determined to make the best of it.

His brother settled in beside me, examining the fittings with the greatest interest, as if he had not been in a carriage of this type before. The groom flicked his whip, and we began to move.

What does one say to a boy of that age? I had no idea, so I spoke as I might to anyone.

"Do you like Paris, Robert?"

"Yes, thank you, sir."

He has Edmund's blue-green eyes, but without the spectacular lashes. He stared at my eye patch before meeting my gaze, and I saw I might learn something from him, if I was prepared to satisfy his curiosity first.

"Some children think I look like a pirate. I am not a pirate, but I have lost a foot and an eye. I stay in Paris to be near my doctors. What brought *you* to France?"

He did not answer but hunched away to cough, pulling out a handkerchief to cover his face. Edmund glanced around. When he saw the boy curled into the corner of the seat, he turned back, but his shoulders were high and tight.

It was a painful sound, the boy's coughing. I guessed its cause, and fear gripped my heart—not for myself, but for him and for Edmund.

The boy's hacking went on for about half a minute. Afterwards, he remained quietly in the same position for a minute or two, as if exhausted. I put my travelling rug over him, and he pulled it up to his neck. Then he raised his head to look out beyond the hood and slowly sat up again.

I despised myself for questioning a sick child and resolved not to do it any more. A passing horseman saluted me, an officer from the Dragoon Guards, and I returned the greeting. When I settled back in my seat, the boy was gazing at my crutches.

"Would you like to see how they work?" I asked. "I would have to get down to show you properly, but one puts them under one's arms, you see, like this, and they take the weight from the legs."

"I should like to try them."

"They would be too long for you. Your feet would not touch the ground."

"Do they make smaller ones for children?"

"Certainly they do."

He contemplated the crutch for a few more moments, and then his eyes slid to my leg—or rather, to my absence of leg. "Does it hurt a great deal?"

We were at the gates now, and the carriage had stopped, waiting to turn. Edmund heard him and twisted round. "Robby!"

The boy's eyes widened. "I am sorry. Was that impertinent? I didn't mean it to be."

"It doesn't matter." I had not minded the question, from him. "My leg doesn't hurt much at present, no. But it often itches, and it hurts if it becomes inflamed."

"My chest is the same. It doesn't hurt every day." He touched the nearest crutch with one finger and said wistfully, "Sometimes I am not allowed to walk, and they push me in a chair. Perhaps I could have these instead?"

"I am afraid not. If the problem is your chest and not your legs, crutches would not help you. You would find them more tiring than walking."

"I see." He regarded me gravely from head to toe. "It was the war, I suppose."

"Yes. A shell exploded near me, and bits of it hit me in different places." It was a long time since I had spoken of the moment that had almost ended my life, and I had never spoken of it in such simple terms. It made it seem . . . not less serious, but less final, less of a tragedy. "It is all getting better."

Robert nodded. "But one can get better without ever getting well."

Indeed, one can.

We had reached a square where the driver pulled up, instructed by Edmund. I leaned forward. "Tell him to go to your door, Vaughan."

"We will not take you any further out of your way, thank you. We are very near, and it has stopped raining." Edmund jumped down and held out his hands. "Come, Robby."

I wanted to keep the child back. The Rue Michel-Ange led off to our right, and I was curious to see where they lived. Robert might invite me in for tea.

But no, Edmund would not allow it. It would throw the household into disarray, no doubt. The mother might not be presentable. There might be no tea—it is more expensive here than in England—and Edmund does not wish me to see inside his life. I must be grateful I was granted the crumb of meeting his young brother.

So I let them go, and the carriage brought me home.

Parkin had lit the lamps and built up the fire, and I enjoyed a hearty tea with muffins—he has discovered a place that bakes in the English way. Afterwards, on a whim, I telephoned Claude, and we went to a supper recital. I came back to a warm, silent apartment with the music still playing in my mind.

"One can get better without ever getting well." The boy must have been ill for a long time, to understand so much.

18

Edmund's Journal
Sunday, February 23rd

The colonel saw us in the Bois and drove us home. It was kind of him, though I wish I had not let him. The rain did not last. It was my fault for taking Robby out when the weather was changeable, but he clamoured to go. It seems cruel that he should spend so long in Paris and see so little of it.

Robby was delighted with the carriage ride. I had warned him he must not discuss our history, so he coughed when asked a question. Unluckily it became a real coughing fit, but he seems none the worse for it. After that they talked about crutches the whole way, he says. I could not always hear above the noise of the hooves and wheels and the driver's muttering, so I can only hope he did not let anything slip out. I cannot imagine how anyone could discuss crutches for ten minutes.

We have saved the minimum we need for Switzerland, and this afternoon's encounter made me think we should go. I said so to Mama this evening. We could then give up these rooms, since I should return alone, and there would be no danger of the colonel questioning Robby again or of anybody recognising Mama.

She did not agree. "I wish we could, but the colonel is likely to engage a new secretary if you go away while he is in the middle of this book, and you will have lost an exceptionally well-paid post. You would be lucky to get such a high salary from anyone else, either here or in London."

I had not thought he would dismiss me if I asked for two weeks' leave. Would he? I am not sure.

"What if you do not find another post?" she went on. "It would be dreadful if we could not pay the sanatorium and had to take Robby away again before the winter."

"I could ask the colonel if he would keep the position open for me. I believe he might."

She put down her sewing. "But think what will happen later in the year, if we go now. Even if he takes you back, all of your salary will go on supporting yourself and paying Robby's fees—and it will still not be enough if I don't find work there at once. With such expenses you will be living hand to mouth. You will certainly not be able to save. Sooner or later, the colonel will finish his book. I expect there will be some revisions, so he may need you until the summer or perhaps the autumn. But then he will let you go, and you will be without employment and without savings at the worst time for Robby, as winter approaches."

I sighed. "I suppose you are right."

She turned her eyes back to her needlework. "I think we should remain here as long as we can. These rooms are much less expensive than the sanatorium. Spring is just around the corner. Robby is always better when the weather improves, and he has become much stronger since we have been able to have Madame's dinners every day instead of living on bread and cheese. It will do him no harm if we stay a few more months. We can add to our savings and be sure of keeping him in Switzerland through next winter."

"Yes, but I am uneasy . . ."

"Really, Edmund, I do not see why. What is the worst that can happen? Suppose the colonel finds out about Charles and dismisses you. Then we shall go, no worse off than if we leave now by our own choice. If he does not, and we stay, we shall be in a much better position by the time your duties come to an end."

Of course, she was right. I was not considering Robby. I was considering only myself. I do not want the colonel to know our history and think badly of me. He disapproved of my living in Ireland during the war—what would he think about Charles?

Her soft eyes gazed into mine, and I saw how lined her face has become since last year.

"I know this is hard for you, Edmund. You should be establishing yourself in a career with better prospects. You should not have to do this tedious work to support Robby."

"Oh, Mama, I did not mean that! The work is not tedious, and I am happy to support Robby. I only pray I can. You are right, it is better that we stay."

She stroked my cheek with the back of her hand. "Then let our aim be to keep him in Switzerland for all of next winter with a little to spare. After that, we must find a way for you to have your own life."

Now the decision is made, I am glad to stay. I will admit it in these pages—I do not want to leave the colonel, even for two weeks. I look forward to my work, to the time I spend in that grand apartment with him and Parkin. I go along the Paris pavements with a skip in my step on those mornings. I hope his book will not be finished for many more months . . .

19

James's Journal
Tuesday, February 25th

"I was interested to meet your brother," I said to Edmund this morning.

He looked at me warily. "I hope he was no trouble to you."

"Oh, not at all, but I am concerned. He is very thin, and his cough sounds serious. Does he have consumption?"

This was too direct for politeness, and Edmund paled, but I had to get at the truth of it.

He swallowed. "He has a tubercular infection, yes."

"You do not share a bed with him, I trust?"

I spent all of yesterday worrying over this. It happens when families are poor, and they have been very poor, I think. Robert's trousers had been let down more than once, and he had rubbed his feet together as if his boots were too tight.

But Edmund leaned forward and clasped his hands. "No, indeed. We have never shared a bed or even a room. My mother would not allow it. Robby sleeps at the top of the house where the air is clearest. We mask our faces when we attend to him and wash our hands afterwards.

We are meticulous about hygiene. You need not fear I might bring the disease here."

"I was not afraid for myself, but for you."

He seemed taken aback, as if he did not know whether to believe me. After a moment he said, "I can only repeat that I am careful."

"Do you have other brothers and sisters?"

His mouth tightened. "No. May I ask you about a word in your last paragraph? I have written 'cosset' in shorthand, but I don't think it can be right."

"Closet?"

"Thank you, yes, that is it."

He will not discuss his family. Why?

The more he refuses, the more I feel I must know — whatever the cost.

Wednesday, February 26th

I am so restless I cannot settle to anything. I went to a gallery and remembered nothing I had seen, and later turned page after page of a volume of philosophy without taking in a single word. Half of my mind is absorbed with thoughts of Edmund at every moment of the day, and all of my mind at night.

If only we could be natural with each other! Then I believe we would be friends, or more — more than I have had with any man, perhaps. But we are both afraid. I am afraid he will leave if I break down the wall he has built between us. He is afraid . . . of what? Of letting someone in, of having someone know him through and through? — but are we not all afraid of that?

Later

I went to see Claude at the Ritz. He was alone and so delighted to see me that he kissed me on both cheeks, instead of kissing the air half an inch from the skin as everyone usually does.

"James, you are looking wonderfully well. The country air has worked miracles."

Country air? The Bois? No, he meant Rignelle. I was there only last week, but the visit has shrunk to insignificance in my mind because Edmund was not a part of it.

He motioned me to a chair near the fire. "Coffee, or a small cognac?" He tipped his head on one side and examined my face. "Cognac, I think." He rang for his manservant, a bent old creature who exudes gloom, and ordered it. "How is your book? When can I see it?"

"Not yet. It is a poor effort. You would tear it to pieces."

"I would do nothing of the kind. If it is good, I will help you find a publisher, then write a review praising it to the heavens. If it is bad, I will fix what can be fixed, then do the same."

I laughed. "A true friend. In any case, it is not finished."

The cognac arrived. I sipped it, and my body welcomed its fiery sparks.

Claude winked. "Ah, it is marvellous to have something warm and wet trickling down one's throat, is it not? And are you content with your secretary?"

I could not tell if he meant anything by speaking of Edmund in the same breath as his other remark, so I ignored the implication, if there was one.

"Yes, he is very conscientious. He will not be distracted from his work, and he helps me a great deal with the planning of the chapters. He thinks me a pitiful creature, I imagine."

"Why should he think that?"

I indicated my leg.

"Oh, that is nothing — or rather, it is not as serious to other people as it is to you. But you, what do you think of him? That is the question. Perhaps not much, since I understand you did not take him to the country with you . . . ?"

He could only have heard that from Louis. "He would not have come. He would have suspected my motives."

"So you wanted to take him?"

"I did not say that."

"And if I offered to introduce you to a charming young man, fresh from Brittany?"

"I would say thank you, but no."

"Ah!" Claude swirled the last of his cognac around the glass, tipped it into his mouth, and smacked his lips. "I see what is your trouble. You are in love."

A hot flush rose to my cheeks. It was idiotic to feel this way, like a blushing schoolboy. "You think I am in love with my secretary?"

A smug smile spread over his face. "I did not say 'with your secretary.' *You* said that."

I gave an angry laugh. "Well, it is ridiculous, in any case. I shall always have to pay, and he is not the type to make that kind of bargain."

"Do not give up hope—and do not put your value so low. The right man would want you without your money."

"I cannot imagine that 'right man.'"

"I can. You need somebody sympathetic, who will take care of you and put up with your stormiest moods, but who will also be firm with you and know when to stand up to you—which is not easy to do because you expect to be always in charge."

"Of course I do. I have been trained to give orders that men will obey without question."

"And look where obeying without question leads," Claude said, gesturing to my leg.

We talked of other things, of music and theatre and government. He wanted to discuss the peace conference, but I dismissed the subject because it angers me. All those old men arguing over national borders make me think of pigs in a trough. As Edmund said to Diana, if only they could have done it that way in 1914 . . . but they did not, and I do not trust them to do it now.

Claude invited me to dinner, but he was expecting other company, and I was not in the mood for that. As I was leaving, he leaned close to my ear and said, "Do not turn away from love because it seems ridiculous, *mon cher*. Love is always ridiculous."

Friday, February 28th

I have taken to working on my book in the library instead of the salon, when Edmund is not here. It is less comfortable there, but I sense some imprint of his presence beside me, keeping me company. Sometimes I even eat there at midday, as Edmund does. I tell Parkin it saves on coal because the fireplace is so much smaller.

When Parkin brought my lunch today, I had covered the table with books, and he had nowhere to put the tray. To make space, I stacked the books in two piles—mine and my uncle's—because I keep them separately on the shelves. I asked Parkin to put some of them back while I began eating the onion soup. Then, quite out of the blue, I thought of the album of erotic drawings and photographs that my uncle kept on the top shelf.

I put down my spoon. How careless of me to have left that in the room where my secretary worked! What if Edmund browsed the shelves and came upon it? He would not know it was not mine.

I had only seen inside it once, when my uncle showed it to me on one of my visits early in the war. But he had a system for the arrangement of his books, and I knew where it would be.

"Parkin, can you get up to the top shelf? Would you fetch down the third book from the left?"

If I had been able, I would have clambered on the furniture, but Parkin would not do something so improper. He pulled out the library steps, climbed up, and passed a book down to me—Plato's *Phaedrus*.

"No, not that one. I said the third from the left."

He leaned aside so I could see the gap in the row of books. He had not made a mistake—he had taken out the third book from the left.

"Plato should not be there." I got up, supporting myself with one hand on the table. "Can you see one with no markings on the spine or the cover?"

He pulled out the fourth book from the left.

"Don't open it," I said sharply. He did not, but passed it to me. "Thank you. You may put this one back where it was." I gave him *Phaedrus* in exchange.

"In the third place?"

"Yes, exactly where you found it. And this one—the unmarked one—have you ever moved it, or opened it, or seen it before?"

"Not that I recall, sir. I don't disturb your books as a rule."

"What about taking them out for dusting? Has that been done lately—while we were in the country, perhaps?"

He shook his head. "I told the daily woman not to come that week, as I wouldn't be here to keep an eye on her. This room hasn't been done out properly in all my time here. I thought we'd have a good spring clean before Easter."

"All right. Thank you, Parkin. Leave the steps out for now."

The soup went cold while I leafed through the album. There was nothing to show whether anyone had opened it since my uncle died. However, books do not move by themselves, and all of the others are in their right places.

If Parkin says he didn't touch it, he didn't. It must have been Edmund. He was here alone for three full days while I was away, and Antoine said he always stayed until six. He cannot have had enough work to occupy all of that time. Naturally he would turn to the bookshelves.

How did he feel when he saw it? Did it excite him or disgust him? I am almost certain his tastes run to men, but *almost* is not enough. How can I find out?

I cannot ignore this. The thought of Edmund enjoying male erotica in my library is driving me half mad.

If I let him know that I have guessed he has seen the book, his reaction will reveal his feelings about it. Perhaps that is all I need to do.

I must do it in a way that shows him there is no shame in desiring other men. Then, if he is willing, I shall bring him to my bedroom and introduce him to the delight that one man can give another.

Tomorrow he may be mine!

Saturday, March 1st

Well, that was not a success. In truth, it was a catastrophe.

I made a grave error. I forgot my missing leg and my Cyclops eye. I assumed that if he was attracted to men, he would be attracted to me. Of course, he is not.

I did not want to open the subject of the top shelf the moment he arrived, so we spent the morning as always, in dictation. He frowned once or twice and said, when I asked, that he had a slight headache, but I did not alter my plans for that. I could not bear to wait until Tuesday.

He went to the library to eat his lunch. I grew more and more agitated at being separated from him. I had no peace of mind and no appetite for food.

At last I heard the typewriter. I forced myself to have patience until he must almost have finished typing up his notes. Then I went in, and he stopped work.

"Sorry to interrupt you." I gestured to a looking glass in the Chinese style that hangs in the library. "I wonder if you would mind taking a few notes about this mirror, while I think of it?"

"Certainly." He reached for his notebook.

"It was my uncle's—my great-uncle's, to be exact, my grandmother's brother. His portrait hangs above the fireplace in the salon. I have reason to be very grateful to him. You know, perhaps, that I inherited this apartment and much of the contents from him? He made me a rich man when I should otherwise have been cut off without a penny. Come, let me show you."

Edmund stood, since I had spoken as if I meant him to follow me to another room. Instead I took him on a tour of the library, though it is not large, and everything could have been described while we were both seated. That, however, would not have suited my purpose.

I pointed out one or two pieces, then stopped by the bookcases, letting one crutch rest against them so I had a free hand. "Some of these are mine, of course, but the top two shelves are all his books. They are in a certain order . . . Oh, but they are not."

As I expected, he followed my gaze up to the book of erotica, which Parkin had replaced for me on the wrong side of *Phaedrus*. Edmund became quite still, as if he had stopped breathing.

So I was right! He had seen it, and he did not appear disgusted, as would a man who did not share my tastes.

I smiled and said softly, "You did not put it back quite where it should be."

His cheeks drained of all colour. His fingers tightened on his notebook, which he held in front of his chest like a shield.

I put my hand on his shoulder. He seemed not to notice. He was still staring up.

"Come to me, my sweet." I leaned forward, intending to kiss his lovely lips and let him know all was well — but he turned his head with the stiffness of a wooden doll, and for a brief moment he met my gaze. The dark lenses of his glasses were between us, but I was close enough to see through them. The horror in his eyes was unmistakeable. He pushed past me, almost knocking me over, and dashed for the door.

My damnable leg! If I could have run after him, I would have — I would have wrestled him to the floor to stop him leaving. But by the time I had picked up my fallen crutch and hobbled out to the corridor, he was gone. No one was in sight but Parkin, carrying a tea tray.

I could do nothing but watch my servant approach and try to calm my racing heart.

Parkin came right up to me before he spoke. "Mr. Vaughan said to excuse him for the rest of the day, if you please, as he wasn't feeling well. I thought he seemed a bit peaky this morning. Do you want your tea in here?" He went into the library and set the tray down. "It's a pity he didn't stay. A nice cup of tea would've done him good."

When I did not answer, his brows drew together with suspicion, and his voice took on an ominous tone. "I hope nothing happened to upset him?"

I sat down before the typewriter and put my head in my hands.

Later

I long to go to his house, but I am sure he would refuse to see me. Nothing would be gained, and something might be lost. I might drive him from me forever. So I have written the briefest note, which he will receive tomorrow.

> Dear Vaughan,
> Please excuse my behaviour today. You have my word that it will not happen again. I trust I will see you on Tuesday and everything will be as usual.
> Yours most sincerely,
> James Clarynton

20

Edmund's Journal
Saturday, March 1st

He knows I have been looking at the book of masculine love! Oh, how I wish I were a thousand miles away! I wanted to throw myself under a tram in one mad moment on the way home, but I remembered Mama and Robby and could not do it. When I understood what he meant—when he said I had not replaced it correctly—I thought I would faint from shame. I now know what it means to wish for the ground to swallow one up. I would have welcomed an earthquake.

The worst of it is that the book was not his, but his uncle's. When my eyes drank in the photographs and drawings, I assumed that ~~James~~ the colonel had also enjoyed them, so the images seemed to create a delicious web of secret links between his desires and mine. But that was all my imagination.

Of course it was not his. How stupid of me not to realise! He cannot reach that top shelf. And what need would he have of such a collection, anyway? It would only interest those who cannot satisfy their desires in real life. His great-uncle must have been a solitary old man. I am young, but I am equally friendless, while James has any man he wants. How he must pity me!

I think he tried to kiss me. He must have expected me to be willing, but I could not be so casual about it. Relations between men are surely immoral, even if they are not criminal here. Besides, my feelings are too strong. A kiss would mean nothing to him, but in me I fear it would unleash a force that could sweep me beyond the shores of reason.

I could not remain in his presence. I fled the library in confusion, told Parkin I was unwell, and came home.

My headache was real, but it was only a slight annoyance at the time. It is worse now, no doubt because of the hours I have spent tormenting myself with the memory of that moment. I go hot and cold thinking of it.

It is Saturday evening, so I have two full days before he will expect me to go back. In that time, I must decide what to do. I shall resign, I think. I cannot imagine ever facing him again. We must go to Switzerland . . . but how will I explain it to Mama?

21

James's Journal
Tuesday, March 4th

Despite my note, ten o'clock came and went, and Edmund did not arrive. Just before eleven there was a knock at the door, and I hurried from the salon windows to the hall, thinking I must have missed him coming down the street — but it was only the new butcher's boy, who had run up the front stairs instead of leaving the meat with Antoine.

Now it is past twelve, and Edmund is still not here. He has never been a minute late before.

How could I have made such a stupid blunder? I knew he was inexperienced, and yet I rushed at him like a cat pouncing on a mouse. Of course he turned tail and ran!

He will come on Thursday. He must.

Thursday, March 6th

Yesterday I did not move from the couch. Nothing could interest me — not food, not music, not this journal, not the telephone, and certainly not chinoiserie. When Parkin brought me some of my notes in an effort to raise my spirits, I threw them at him. He collected them up from the floor without a word and took them back to the library, leaving me alone to wallow in the darkness of my thoughts.

After breakfast this morning, as I moved restlessly between the door and the windows waiting for some sight or sound of Edmund, a note arrived in a feminine hand.

Dear Colonel Clarynton,
Please excuse my son from his work this week. He is not well.
Yours sincerely,
E. A. Vaughan (Mrs.)

Relief flooded through me. He had not resigned, nor was he staying away because he could not bear to see me! He was ill, that was all.

Or was it an excuse? No, it must be true, or he would have written himself. He is always so upright—he would not ask his mother to lie on his behalf.

And he'd had a headache that morning. He had already told me so. Perhaps he is one of those unfortunate people who have sick-headaches that last for several days. The pain might have been increasing all the day, with my clumsy approach and his embarrassment about the erotic book adding the final straw.

What a despicable trick I played on him with that book! How could I have acted so selfishly? All my manoeuvring to discover his secrets has been nothing but a cruel game. I cannot believe I showed so little respect for his feelings, so little courtesy. Parkin was kinder to him . . .

and that, no doubt, is why he tells Parkin things he will not tell me.

I informed Parkin of the contents of the note. I had opened it in his presence, and I could not resist sharing my joy at the knowledge that Edmund has not left us. Parkin remained as grave as always, but he does not have the feelings for Edmund that I do, and he did not know what I had done or how I had feared losing Edmund.

I rang for Parkin again a moment ago.

"Did Mr. Vaughan ever mention headaches before?"

"I don't believe so, sir. More coffee?"

"No, you can clear it away. I am agitated enough."

"Dr. De Smet's secretary telephoned to remind you he is coming about your eye at two o'clock."

"Yes, yes. Very well. I shall not go out."

Now I hobble to the windows—a wet day, but nothing can dampen my spirits. Paris goes about its business on the streets below. Edmund does not hate me. All is life and hope and bustle.

I take up the note again. Another E. Vaughan! What is this one, I wonder? Edna, Ethel, Emily? Females enjoy more variety in their names. I cannot hope to guess it.

She writes a ladylike hand, but so brief. Substitute *school* for *his work* and it is something she might have written to his headmaster a few years ago—rather amusing!

I must reply. I shall do that now to say of course he is excused, and I look forward to seeing him when he is recovered.

Later

De Smet came. He thinks my socket will take a glass eye without difficulty, but I must have another small surgical procedure first. Before he can do that, every sign of the old infection must be gone. He will come again in a fortnight, and if all is well, he will give me an appointment for the operation.

No visitors have appeared to fill the dull space between tea and dinner, and my mood has darkened with the fading of the light. I have reread Mrs. Vaughan's note, and it no longer amuses me.

Why didn't Edmund write himself? Is he too ill to hold a pen?

Friday, March 7th

I could not sleep for worrying. It is now six days since Edmund was here. Would a simple sick-headache last so long? Might it not be something more serious?

When Parkin brought my tea this morning, I pushed myself up to a sitting position. "I am concerned about this illness of Mr. Vaughan's."

"Yes, sir"—in a tone that suggested he shared my concern.

"I have thought of visiting, but he would not like it."

Parkin did not reply. He was fussing with my shaving things, so I could not see his face.

It cost me a great deal to add, "I believe he would prefer to see you."

He moved to the chest where he keeps my underclothes. "Gentlemen in reduced circumstances often do not like to receive visitors of their own class, sir."

That consoled me a little. "Yes. He has his pride." I watched him put a single sock on the chair—I no longer need them to be kept in pairs. "You think he is of my class, then?"

"Not quite, perhaps, but I would hesitate to place him anywhere else."

"A natural gentleman?"

As I said it, I saw the double meaning. Could he be illegitimate? It would explain the absence of a father. So many families are without fathers since the war, however, that it scarcely needs explaining.

I returned to the plan I had formed in the night.

"I should have liked to see for myself how he is, but I think it is better if you go, Parkin. I will give you the address—it is in Auteuil—and you may take a cab, of course. Fill a basket with eggs and chicken or whatever Henri can offer to tempt his appetite. If you find he needs a doctor, and his mother hesitates because of the expense, you may call one on my account."

Parkin went immediately after breakfast. I gave him Edmund's salary for this week and last, since I had not paid him when he left so abruptly on Saturday. They may need it.

That was an hour ago. Parkin may be back soon. I shall go to the window and watch for him.

Later

My spirits sank when I saw Parkin alight from the cab carrying the basket with care, as if it was still full of eggs. It was covered, and I told myself that perhaps Mrs. Vaughan had sent a gift in return. But no, Parkin had not found them.

I listened to his explanation in silence.

"They don't live at number thirty-eight and never have. The chap in the shop there thinks they're somewhere near. I walked about a bit and enquired at some houses that had rooms to let, but nobody had heard of an English family called Vaughan. It's an area where foreigners are ten a penny and every other house offers lodgings, although a lot of them had the shutters up." He gave me the bundle of francs. "You'd better lock this away again, sir."

I stared at the money in my hands without seeing it. "If it is the wrong address, why were my notes to Vaughan and his mother not returned?"

"It's what they call an accommodation address — a stationer's shop where they take in letters for people to collect. The man brought them out when I asked, and there were two for the Vaughans. It looked like your stationery, though I couldn't see the writing to make sure. From what I understood, Mr. Vaughan calls in most days as a general rule, but he hadn't been in this week. The chap said very likely Mr. Vaughan's not well, but we knew that. Here, sir, you're getting those all crumpled. Shall I put them in the bureau for you?"

"Yes, thank you." I gave him my keys and opened my fist to let him take the banknotes. I had crushed them to a ball.

They have not collected their letters this week. If Edmund is not well enough, why would his mother not go, or his brother, or someone else from their house?

Have they gone? Moved away from Auteuil—or left Paris?

I telephoned Mrs. Bullock at the American Red Cross. I told her the truth—not all of it, of course, but that his mother had written to say he was ill so I had sent my man with provisions, and he had not been able to find them.

"I wonder if I have made a mistake with the address," I said. "Would you be so good as to look in your files? I have thirty-eight Rue Michel-Ange."

She went away, and drawers clattered. A rustle of papers, then, "Yes, we have the same."

I had not expected that. I thought he only had secrets from me. But no, he had also hidden from the Red Cross.

She went on, "I guess they moved, and he forgot to give you the new address. How's he getting along?"

"Very well. His work is excellent. I must thank you—you taught him his shorthand, I believe."

"I can't say we did that. We lent him the books and he taught himself. But we trained him in American efficiency!" She gave a rumbling laugh, but quickly sobered. "I hope you will have him back soon, but if he has the Spanish flu, don't expect much from him for three or four weeks. I've had several workers go down with it, and they don't recover fast. One didn't recover at all."

The influenza! It had not crossed my mind. Thousands of people in Paris died last year — not the old, the sick, and the weak, as with the usual kind of flu, but healthy men and women like Edmund . . .

My trembling arm could barely hold the receiver. "I thought the epidemic had ended."

"Oh no, it's not over yet. It was at its worst right around the armistice, but it hung on all winter and had a second peak last month." She quoted me hospital admission figures and death rates until I wished her on the other side of the Atlantic.

Edmund, no . . .

I have not prayed since I was a schoolboy, but I am praying now.

Do not let him die! Let him have left Paris — let him live all his long life without my ever seeing him again, rather than that!

22

James's Journal
Saturday, March 8th

I went to see Claude and told him everything.

He patted my hand. "Do not worry, *mon cher*. The Spanish flu kills very fast. If it began last Saturday, and he was still alive for his mother to write on Wednesday or Thursday, I think he will survive."

Did he expect that to comfort me? "But I do not know when it began. He might have become ill on Tuesday. The headache might have been nothing."

"Or he might have the migraine, as you first thought, and not the Spanish flu at all."

His servant came in with coffee. When it was served, I said, "I must find him. Would you ask Mrs. Bullock if there is any other clue in her file, anything at all? She recommended him to you, did she not? You must know her better than I do. She might tell you, but not me."

"No. Madame Bullock, I barely know her. It was not she who recommended your secretary — at least, not at first. She did when I asked her about him, yes, but the first person to give me his name was someone else at the Red Cross, a friend of mine. I will ask him to look, if he has not returned to New Jersey. I shall be happy to have a reason to speak to him again."

Despite my worry, I was intrigued. "You have never mentioned an American friend."

Claude did not meet my gaze. "Have a madeleine. They are still warm."

He held the plate out to me. I took one, but I had no appetite for cakes. "Please do not change the subject, Claude."

"Very well. I did not tell you about him because he is a quacker, and I thought you would not like it."

"A— Oh, a Quaker? You mean he was a conchie, a pacifist?" I set down my cup and pushed away my plate. "Once I would have minded, perhaps, but I do not care any more. The conchies were brave in their own way ... and the war is over."

My attitude to men who did not fight has reversed in recent months. Once I was suspicious of Edmund because he spent the war in Ireland. Now I thank God he was spared the horror.

So Claude will ask his American friend to delve into the files of the Red Cross.

At every post I tear the letters from Parkin's hand, hoping to see one from Edmund and dreading another from his mother, in case— But I cannot write it.

Nothing has come from either of them.

Claude is silent too. What if his friend has gone back to the United States? No, Claude would have discovered that by now, and told me.

But even if the fellow is still here, somebody whose conscience objected to war might also object to prying in the Red Cross files. I hope Claude can persuade him ...

Monday, March 10th

Claude telephoned at last, soon after lunch. His friend had agreed to look, and at midday he had had an opportunity to search Mrs. Bullock's office.

"There is nothing in the file, I am sorry," Claude said. "Only the address you already knew, in the Rue Michel-Ange. But he remembered something. He saw your secretary's passport once, when the police wanted to inspect documents from all employees, and he had another name, like the Spaniards do."

"A Spanish name?"

"No, another name after Vaughan. He has several names, like the Spaniards. They are called José or whatever it may be, then they have their father's surname, then their mother's. And sometimes they use only the father's name, which is the one before the last. There are many Spaniards in the USA — or I suppose they are Mexicans — so my friend is used to this custom and was not surprised to see your secretary doing the same."

I could make no sense of this. "Do you mean Edmund goes by his mother's surname?"

"No — at least, I do not know. Stop interrupting and let me tell you. He has several names, and Vaughan is not the last one. That is all I meant. The last name was Ingram, my friend thinks. He is not sure because he saw it only once, six months ago, but he thinks so."

I twisted the telephone cord between my fingers. "So Vaughan is one of his middle names, and his last name is Ingram?"

"Yes, Edmund Vaughan Ingram, or something like that. But he was called always Edmund Vaughan, as José María González García might be called José González. Is that useful?"

No wonder Parkin had not found the Vaughan family by knocking on doors, if that was not their real name!

"Yes. Oh, yes. Thank you, Claude. If I can ever do anything for you . . ."

He laughed. "You have already done it, *mon cher*. As I told you, I was pleased to have a reason to talk to my American friend again."

I replaced the receiver and went to the pantry, where Parkin was polishing the silver.

"Does the name *Ingram* mean anything to you, Parkin?"

He held a knife up to the light. "In what connection, sir?"

"As if it might be a name that somebody might not wish known. Some scandal associated with it, perhaps, or a crime — in England during the war, most likely. I would have missed it then. You heard all the society gossip in your last employment, I imagine, and read the newspapers?"

"Yes, sir, but nothing comes to mind."

"If it should, let me know, will you?"

*

He told me after dinner. He let me eat, and then, when he was pouring my brandy, he said, "That name you were asking me about, sir..."

My heart thumped. "Yes?"

"Well, there was a Captain Ingram, only it wasn't spelled the way you might expect. It was I-N-G-R-E-H-A-M. And it was in the nineties, not in the war. Might that be it?"

It could be Edmund's father or some other close relation. "Perhaps. What did he do?"

"He was a swindler — cheated at cards — and as you'll know, that's about the worst thing an army officer could have done in those days. He'd been to the house once, the house where I was, that is, and the duke was most put out that he'd entertained this bounder, as he called him."

"Mm." The man would have had reason to use another name. But even if he was Edmund's father, the offence did not seem serious enough to explain Edmund's fear of discovery twenty or thirty years later. "He left England, I suppose, this Captain Ingreham?"

"Oh yes, and he took a lady with him, an earl's daughter. She ran off with him. There was a terrible scandal. She was already married, you see."

Now we were beginning to get to it. "Do you remember her name?"

"Lady Elizabeth Mannington. She'd visited us too, before it all happened."

"Mannington? What earldom is that?"

"That was her married name, sir. Her husband wasn't titled. I don't recall her maiden name, but she was a daughter of Lord Akingbourne, I think."

"Ah." I did not know the family, but I had an idea there was a son who had done something brave at the Somme and got killed doing it. "Thank you, Parkin."

I went to the library and took down one of my uncle's reference books to look up Lord Akingbourne. The volume is dated 1906, but I have nothing more recent.

AKINGBOURNE, *fifth earl, John Frederick William Vaughan-Herewick, S. 1904; b. 6 April 1866, s. of the Hon. Frederick George David Vaughan-Herewick; m. 1890 Lucinda Joanna Harcourt, d. of Sir Wm. Harcourt, 1st Baronet; two s. Address: Akingbourne Hall, Akingbourne, Glos.*

I found the village of Akingbourne in the atlas. It is not far from Diana's parents' place. I tried to get her on the telephone, but she was out.

The family name is Vaughan-Herewick. Is that where Edmund's "Vaughan" comes from? I wondered for a moment if he might be one of the *two s.*, two sons. But then his legal name would be Vaughan-Herewick, not Ingreham.

No, the scandal could not have been in this branch of the family. Lady Elizabeth must have been a daughter of the previous earl.

I tried Ingreham.

INGREHAM, *Capt. Charles Edgar, late of Royal Irish Lancers; b. 25 November 1867; m. 1900 Lady Elizabeth Amelia Mannington, div. wife of P. E. Mannington, Esq., and d. of Charles Robert Arthur Vaughan-Herewick, fourth earl of Akingbourne; two s.*

No address for Captain Ingreham, but the Irish regiment was suggestive. Edmund had told me at our interview that he was born in Ireland. The *E. A. Vaughan (Mrs.)* on the note I had received could well be an alias for Lady Elizabeth Amelia Ingreham, previously Mannington, née Vaughan-Herewick. Again, there are two sons, who could be Edmund and Robert. Robert must be a little older than I thought, if he was born before this book was published in 1906, but consumptive children are often small for their age.

I can see how Lady Elizabeth might now be living in poverty in Paris, dependent on her elder boy. Her father, who died in 1904 when the new earl succeeded, would very likely have disinherited her. In any case, the Akingbourne estate would have gone with the title, and her father might not have had much else to leave. The fifth earl is not her brother, from whom she could have hoped for support, but a cousin, a son of her father's younger brother. As for her second husband, Captain Ingreham, he might have died too, since this book was published.

After her scandalous elopement — with a swindler, a cheat, when she was already married — and the birth of Edmund in 1897, before her marriage to Ingreham, one sees why she would not wish to be known.

And I had imagined Edmund the son of a virtuous clergyman!

I rested my elbows on the desk and stared at the print for a long time, trying to conjure up Edmund's life between the lines. I should have been excited about all these discoveries, but I was not. The story was too sad.

Am I jumping to conclusions? I cannot be sure this is his family. I only have the similarity of Ingreham and

Ingram to go on, and the name of Vaughan, and her initials. All of those could be coincidental.

But it would fit with his behaviour. It would mean the secrets he is protecting are not his own but his mother's. That would explain why he defends them so fiercely.

I could find out. I could ask Claude to ask his friend if the name might have been spelled *Ingreham*. But does it matter?

They must be using the stationer's to receive letters in the name of Vaughan because at the house where they live, they are known by their real name. Even now, one cannot take rooms in Paris without showing a passport or identity card. During the war, when every foreigner not in uniform was suspected of being a spy, it would have been out of the question to try.

So I know enough to track them down. If I hired a dozen men to go to every door in Auteuil asking for Madame Ingreham or Ingram, I would find them if they are still there, and I might discover where they have gone if they have left.

This is what I have dreamed of — finding him and bringing him back to me. Yet I hesitate. I do not want to set a pack of hounds to hunt Edmund down and drag him here. I want to hear his knock at my door, asking admittance. I want him to come back to me of his own free will.

I shall wait.

23

Edmund's Journal
Undated

I do not know how much time has passed since I last wrote in these pages.

I have had the Spanish flu and almost died. It is a terrible sickness, not like any influenza I have known before. One turns blue and coughs up vile stuff, as if all the blood has left the arteries to fill the lungs instead. Many people drown in it. That is one way it kills.

For several days and nights, I could not sleep for coughing. I have a pain at the base of the ribs, which Mama was afraid was a sign of pneumonia. That would have finished me for sure. The doctor says, however, that I have only strained a muscle from coughing so much.

He wanted to send me to hospital, but Mama would not let him. She said that other diseases lurk on the wards to strike the weak, the nurses have little time for each patient, and nothing is done for influenza in hospitals that could not be done better at home. It is true, I think, if one has a healthy person to nurse one, as I had Mama.

She has caught it now and has taken to her bed. I shall nurse her as she nursed me.

Robby has no symptoms, for which we thank God. So far, the masks we wear to protect us from his illness have protected him from ours. I pray they will continue to do so.

No food or hot water had reached us for days, so I went downstairs this morning, gripping the banister lest my weak legs gave way. I found Mme. H. lying on her couch. She, too, is recovering, but she was laid low by grief. The flu has been all through the house, and the poor woman has lost her daughter to it, though her grandchild was spared and has gone to other family.

Without the child to feed, she had done no shopping and did not seem likely to, so I went out. The streets looked as they did in the bombardment last year, when the German lines were so close — shops shut up, few people about. Those who were out hurried past without speaking, scarves over their faces to protect against contagion.

We all thought the epidemic was over, but it has lashed our little district with the sting in its tail.

I went to the baker's, but the shutters were closed. A woman leaned out of an upstairs window in the next house to tell me the baker's family had had the flu first. She cursed them, saying they had coughed on their customers and spread the disease all through the *quartier*. The baker died, the rest of the family have gone, and the next nearest baker's is also closed, she told me. If I wanted bread, I must go another kilometre for it.

I had not the strength to walk so far, so I went to the butcher's and ordered a pot of good broth to be made fresh each day and delivered by their boy. They charged three times what I expected, but I paid it.

Colonel Clarynton is to thank for my survival, I think. Without the generous salary he pays, we would not have been as strong and well fed as we are. Some of the money for Switzerland will have to go on the doctor's fees and the medicines, but at least we can buy what we need. Many others cannot.

I also called at the stationer's, where I found two notes from my employer. One was sent the evening of the day I last saw him, asking me to excuse his behaviour. At first I could not think what behaviour he meant. I suppose it is the moment when he tried to kiss me, if that is what he did. I am surprised he felt the need to apologise or to write at all. My shame over his uncle's book seems unimportant now, as if it happened long ago in another country, to someone else.

His other letter was addressed to Mama, who asked me to open it for her. It is dated a few days later and says that I may take all the time I need to get well. She wrote when I wanted to get up and go back to him. She had trouble restraining me until she could swear that she had sent my excuses and he would not expect me.

I am glad to have these letters. I was afraid he might have caught the influenza from me that day — he stood so close — but his hand is as firm as ever in the second note, so I think he is safe.

I have replied to say I will return as soon as we are all free of infection, if he has not engaged someone else in my absence. I must not go yet, for fear of carrying the sickness from our house to his.

When I came back from posting my letter, the boy was here with the broth. He put it on the step and went back across the road, waiting there to see me take it in. It is like living in a plague house.

Mme. H. got up and boiled some potatoes to make the broth go further. Robby and I are well enough for those, and we were famished! Mama can swallow nothing solid.

I asked Mme. H. if we should feed the other families in the house. She said the young couple below us are in hospital, and the Russians on the first floor have shut themselves in to avoid infection. They will not touch anything that is left for them. She believes they are living on sausages and beer.

Mama is stirring. I shall try to make her take a little more broth.

24

James's Journal
Tuesday, March 11th

At last, a note from Edmund in his own hand, somewhat shakier than usual. It was the influenza, my greatest fear . . . but he has fought it off! He is well again and will come back to me when the risk is gone.

I cannot contain my joy. I attempted to waltz with Parkin, crutches and all.

Every day I have hoped and dreaded to hear what had become of him. Mrs. Bullock frightened me more badly than I cared to admit.

The letter makes no mention of anything that happened between us. It is too much to expect that he has forgotten, but he has forgiven, perhaps, and we can start afresh when he returns.

Later

I have been to see Diana. Having thrown off my anxiety, I could not resist the temptation to find out more about Lady Elizabeth and the family at Akingbourne.

I had to be patient, however, because she was bursting with her own news. She is engaged — to Johnny.

"I had almost made up my mind to have Bill," she said, "but he gave a dinner for me, and I heard him telling Lucie de Treguille the same story he had already told me and Admiral Carter and Margery Bullock, in the same words. It is a story that reflects rather well on him about something he did under fire, and I suddenly pictured him in my mind, as clear as I see you now, at the age of sixty, red-faced and clutching a glass, telling that same old war story over and over, with nobody left to listen to it but me. I could not face it."

"So that was the end of Bill?"

"It was."

"Have you told Johnny the good news?"

"Of course." She showed me the ring. It surprised me.

"Is it silver?"

"Oh, James, of course not!" She laughed. "It is the latest thing—a diamond hoop set in platinum. Gold is so *passé*."

I took her hand and brought it closer to my eye. The diamonds were not large, but they were fine.

"He has good taste."

"I should hope so. After all, he has chosen me."

We both laughed at that. Her laughter is like the rippling of a stream.

"We shall tie the knot next month in London," she went on. "I want to be married in England, and one can do it more simply in town than in the country. As it is my second marriage, I do not need all the fuss. Might you come?"

"I think not. The doctors want me here, so they can experiment with false eyes and legs." I will not go back to

England while my father is alive . . . but I have not told her this.

"That is a pity. Are you sure? Then I may not see you for some time. We leave almost immediately for the publication of the banns. Afterwards he wants to go to America to find out about their automobiles. So we shall spend our honeymoon in Detroit, of all places, but I have insisted on a week in New York at each end. Then we will return to England, and he will build his own vehicles and make his fortune."

"What if he loses a fortune instead?"

"Then we will live in blissful poverty!" She laughed again. "No, really, I have enough to support us, if we are careful. And it is paid by trustees, so I cannot be tempted to take it all and sink it in gears and axles or whatever he will need."

"I shall miss you," I said. And indeed Paris without Diana will be like an apple tree when the frost has nipped its blossom—still fruitful, but not what it might have been.

"You're too sweet." She patted my arm. "Don't worry, I shall be back twice a year for the fashions, if the money holds out—and once a year, even if it doesn't! And of course you must come and see us when you have all your new parts."

"You make me sound like one of his motor cars." I shifted my weight—my shoulder was painful again—and brought the subject rather clumsily to the Ingrehams. "So you will not be married in Gloucestershire? By the way, do you know the family at Akingbourne? I heard a story the other day—"

She interrupted me. "Oh, yes! That was such a tragedy. They are not far from us at all. I have known them all my life. They had two boys, Freddy and David, about our age. No other children. And they were both killed at the Somme in the same week. The telegrams came one day and the next. Can you imagine? You have barely taken in the news of the first, you pass a terrible night, and then another telegram arrives... They thought at first it must be a duplicate, a second message about David, but no, Freddy was gone too."

"Dreadful." Those must have been the sons of the fifth earl. I did not want to dwell on them—too painful. I had heard a hundred such stories, but one never becomes completely hardened. "And wasn't there something in the previous generation, some scandal?"

"There was, yes. The last earl had two daughters, and one of them, Elizabeth, ran off with a cad. Daddy grew up with those girls, as I grew up with the boys. In fact, when she eventually hit rock bottom, it was Daddy who convinced Lord Akingbourne—the new one—to support her. But that ended last year, of course, when Charles Ingreham was shot for desertion."

"Shot for desertion?" My heart thumped, and I sat upright. I thought of the entry in my uncle's reference book. *INGREHAM, Capt. Charles Edgar.* Edmund's father?

"Don't you remember?" Diana said. "It wasn't in the papers, but people were talking about it because executions were rare so late in the war."

"I didn't hear anything. When was it exactly?"

"Sometime last summer... July or August. Oh, you must have been hit about then. You came through to us in August, didn't you?"

She was right. I'd have been at the clearing station, in pain I had not known a man could live through, wishing the shell had blown off my head.

Diana took a cigarette, and I lit it for her. She said, "Everything has gone wrong for that family. Elizabeth was already married when she bolted with the Ingreham fellow, and her first husband refused to divorce her for a long time. She had two boys, born out of wedlock — or rather, in the wrong wedlock, because in law they were her first husband's responsibility. Eventually the husband must have seen the disadvantage of this, and he divorced her, so she and Ingreham were able to marry. I suppose Ingreham adopted the boys, and I think there was another child. Soon after that, he left her."

"*Two* boys before she remarried? Are you sure?"

She and Ingreham had married in 1900, according to the directory. Robert could not have been born before that — he is certainly not nineteen. So there must have been another brother, if this was Edmund's family.

Diana nodded. "Fairly sure. Charles and another one before they married, and a third later. Why all the interest?"

"*Charles*? So who was the deserter? The father — the man Elizabeth ran off with?"

"No, the eldest son. The father was out of the picture by then. He went off before the war, to the Argentine, I think."

The eldest son! Edmund's older brother, a deserter!

I began the war thinking all deserters should be shot. I had changed my mind before the end—they were pitiful creatures, and prison was enough—but this news unbalanced me, all the same. I would have minded less if it were his father, illogical though that may be.

But brother or father, the important thing is that it was not Edmund himself. I shall not think any less of him for it.

Diana was still talking, going over the story again. "They lived in Italy mostly, until Ingreham senior bailed out. The old earl had died by then, leaving Elizabeth nothing in his will. When she found herself alone with the children and no money, she went home. Her sister would not help, so she threw herself on the mercy of her cousin, the new earl."

She tapped ash from her cigarette. "This must have been about 1909. I was not supposed to know because it was such a scandal, but I heard Daddy and Mummy discussing it. Mummy thought she should be turned away, but Daddy said she had suffered enough, so he spoke to Lord Akingbourne. She was given an income on which to live quietly—in England, I think, but not in Gloucestershire. That lasted until the son was court-martialled, found guilty, and shot. Akingbourne was horrified to discover he had supported a deserter. Bad luck on her, to lose her income just at that time, but one can hardly blame Akingbourne after what happened to his sons."

This made me certain it was Edmund's family. Lady Elizabeth's financial support ended with her son's execution last summer, and Edmund started work at the Red Cross in August. The names, the dates, his unwillingness to tell me if he had lost anyone in the war — it could not be coincidence.

Diana crossed her ankles and examined the toe of her shoe. "I have no idea how she lives now. She may take in laundry, for all I know, or perhaps the second son is old enough to go for a clerk."

This was too close to the truth for my peace of mind. I turned the subject back to her wedding, but I was still in turmoil when I came home.

My poor Edmund — what he has been through! The stain of the old scandal, his father leaving them, his younger brother with consumption, the disgrace and execution of his older brother, and finally the loss of the family income.

I wish he could have told me himself. I wish he had felt he could confide in me. But it is my own fault that he did not, with all the fuss I made about his spending the war in Ireland.

Should I tell him I know, when he returns? I cannot decide.

25

Edmund's Journal
Wednesday, March 12th

We have lost Mama.

I thought writing those words might make it seem real, but it does not. It cannot be real. It is not possible.

I assumed it would be the same for her as for me — she would cough a great deal and then recover. I did not imagine for a moment that God would take her from us.

When I last wrote, she seemed to be getting better. But yesterday she began to sink again, and the fight went out of her. Still I never doubted. I only thought it might take her a little longer to get well.

I found her this morning at dawn. I was there all night with her, but I had fallen asleep in the chair. I hope she did not wake. I cannot bear to think of her trying to call in her last moments and having no answer.

Robby went very pale when I told him, but he has taken it bravely. He is the strong one just now.

I do not know what to do about the funeral. I wish someone could be there, so that Robby and I would not be alone. Perhaps Mme. H. will come, despite disapproving of our Anglican church.

If only we did not have so many secrets! Then I could ask James — I should not call him that — and Parkin, and

Mrs. Bullock. But it cannot be. I must not even write to our aunt or our cousin yet, because I promised Mama that if this happened, I would tell no one at all until afterwards. She will be buried under our real name, of course, and she did not want me to be recognised and lose my post. I made the promise to reassure her, never thinking I would be called upon to keep it.

We will not have it announced in the papers, but I am afraid people may hear about it anyway, because there are so few English churches in Paris. Will the chaplain think it odd if I ask him to say nothing to anyone? If word gets out that Mama was here and has died, Lady Diana Grantleigh might come despite the old scandal, since her father knew Mama so well. She might even ask James to accompany her. Very likely they know Charles was her son, and I could not bear to see James's face when he understood who I was — not there, not then.

Then there is the cost. However small the funeral, it will eat into the money we had saved. I must pay the doctor too. And how will we manage without Mama to care for Robby? He is not always well enough to be left alone all day while I work. How will I ever save up again, if he needs a nurse?

It is despicable to think of money at such a time . . . but the money is not for me, it is for Robby.

There is one thing I can do, if things become desperate — if I dare.

But if I do that, I must first tell James the truth, and very likely that will be the end of it. Perhaps I will think of some other way when I am stronger.

I wish I had told Mama more about my feelings for James. She knew the world, and she might have understood better than I imagined. But it is too late, and I have no one to advise me now. I feel so alone.

If only we had left last month!

Oh, Mama—

26

James's Journal
Tuesday, March 18th

Edmund came back to work today, looking thinner than I have ever seen him. He was not wearing his dark glasses, but his eyes were so dull, I could not delight in them.

"I was awfully sorry to hear about your mother," I said as soon as we were settled in the library. "Thank you for writing to let me know."

He did not answer but bent to take the cover off the typewriter, so I could not see his face.

I began, "Is the funeral—"

"It was on Friday."

That was a pity. I had intended to tell him I knew who his mother was and ask if my presence might be welcome—or at least not unwelcome. But it was too late.

"If there is anything I can do...?"

"There is nothing anyone can do." He turned away to gather his notebook and pencil. "If you don't mind, I would rather not talk about it. I am ready to start work."

I dictated a few paragraphs, leaving him with that and the corrected pages from when he was last here.

At lunch I asked Parkin, "How do you find Mr. Vaughan?"

"He's doing his best, sir, but I think he's very tired."

"You might ask him if he needs a loan for the funeral expenses and so on. I tried to give him his salary, and he refused payment for the weeks he was ill, so I know he will not accept anything else from me. But perhaps he would take it from you. I would make sure you were not out of pocket."

Parkin coughed. "I already took the liberty, sir. He was grateful for the offer, but he told me he's been able to save while he's been working here, and it's all paid for."

I thought of the young man sitting alone with his grief in the library, preferring to confide in Parkin than in me, and I felt more helpless than I have since I was first wounded. It was a joy to me to have him back, but I did not believe it was a joy to him to be here.

I came to a decision. "Tell him my shoulder aches, I can do nothing else today, and he had better go home when he has had his lunch."

"*Yes*, sir."

It is rare for Parkin to look pleased with me, but he did at that moment.

Saturday, March 22nd

I have had the final operation on my eye socket, and all is well, but it needs six weeks to heal and settle.

Diana has left for London.

Edmund continues to come, and we have settled back into our regular habits. I believe we must rework the draft completely, following the same plan.

I am doing what I can to bring him back to full health. Parkin told me he never eats more than half of his lunch, so we have chocolate in the mornings instead of coffee, and tempting delicacies at tea. The cake plate comes out of the library emptier than it went in, but I suspect Edmund carries the slices away for his young brother. My waistcoat is getting tight, while he remains as thin as a reed and as fragile.

I should like to tell him I know about his history, but I am afraid of driving him away. What keeps him in Paris? He might take his brother back to England if I press too hard, and I could not follow him there.

27

Edmund's Journal
Sunday, March 23rd

Something is broken in me.

I have been back at work for a week, and there is a constraint between me and James that was never there before. Between me and Robby, too; between me and Parkin. Between me and the world.

I am shut in a glass box, with people tapping on it, trying to get my attention.

Robby said to me today that we should go for a promenade in the Bois. He thought it would do me good. A few weeks ago, I recall saying that to him. Somehow we have changed places.

As we went through the gates, I caught myself watching the passing carriages for two black horses pulling a Victoria with crutches propped against the seat. But he did not come.

Robby needed to rest sooner than I expected. Even though he was spared the influenza, this winter has taken its toll on him. The doctor said something about this the last time he came, but I had not wanted to think about it. I could not take in any more bad news then. My mind would not accept it.

We sat on the grass, and he said, "What will we do, Edmund?"

"What would you like to do? The cascade is too far, but we could walk by the big lake, perhaps, or go to the hippodrome to look at the horses."

Robby gave me a look of pity. "I don't mean today. I mean what will we *do*?"

"Oh." A family walked by with five children in a line, arranged by height. "I don't know. It is hard to decide."

"I don't think you should decide by yourself," Robby said in his firmest voice. "You should talk to me about it."

Should I? How much can a boy of eleven understand? He knows he has tuberculosis. He must fear he will die. If I were him, I would want to know for sure. But nobody knows what Robby's future holds. We can only do what the doctors say, and hope.

When I did not reply, he added, "I am not as well as I was before."

I did not like the tremor in his voice, but I told him the thing I had not previously faced. "The doctor says your lungs have become more vulnerable. It doesn't mean . . . it doesn't mean you won't get better. But you shouldn't stay much longer in a city like Paris or London. There is too much smoke. Earlier in the year, he thought we could safely remain here until the end of the summer, but now he says not. You need cleaner air."

"He thinks I should go to Switzerland now?"

"Yes, or to a sanatorium somewhere else. It might not be in Switzerland. They exist in France and England too."

Robby pulled at the grass beside his legs. "Why would I go to one in France or England instead of Switzerland?"

The void that lay in the place of my heart grew deeper and darker. I did not want to accept the truth myself, but I had to tell him. I took a breath. "It is difficult to see how we can do it, without Mama."

"You mean the cost? Won't our cousin pay?"

"No, Robby. You know he stopped supporting us."

"I knew he'd stopped her allowance, but I thought he would still . . ." He stared off into the distance.

Mama must have let him believe Lord Akingbourne would cover his sanatorium fees. I had not known this, or I would have broken the news more gently.

"Then how would I have gone?" he asked at last. "Is this why she talked of dressmaking—she would have worked to pay the fees?"

"She and I between us."

"You too? Always?"

"Until you got well, yes."

He hugged his knees and sat looking at the sky. Small white clouds scudded across the blue, but they were high. The weather would not change today.

He sighed. "I suppose if the sanatorium she chose for me is the best, it must also be expensive."

I could not deny it. I doubt we could have managed to pay the fees on our own for very long if she had lived, but she had been determined to try. Perhaps she had hoped our cousin's heart would soften in time.

I said, "The problem is that I do not earn enough by myself, even if I used every franc the colonel pays me."

"And you cannot do that, because you have to eat and sleep somewhere." He turned to me with his jaw set firm. "So we must find a cheaper sanatorium. Perhaps one in

France at first, because you need to stay in Paris to finish the colonel's book." His expression clouded. "You will visit me, won't you?"

"Of course." I forced myself to smile. "We might find a clinic that's close enough for me to come every week."

No doubt we could, since we cannot afford a place in the healthy mountain air. But I should not have said it. The train fares . . .

A little black dog walked by, a ball of fluff no bigger than a kitten, pulling a large lady on a long lead. Robby pointed to them and laughed. Even when we are discussing something so serious, he keeps his sense of humour. I shall miss him if he leaves Paris.

He is all I have.

He reached out to me as if he had read my mind, gripping my thumb the way he used to years ago when I first walked him to school. We sat for a minute or two like that, and then we went on to the hippodrome.

He thinks we have made a decision, but I cannot send him to some third-rate clinic in the damp lowlands of northern France. Nor can I keep him here in the smoky city air.

I shall tell James everything and make my proposal. It does not seem risky any more. I shall be speaking from within the glass box, where nothing can hurt me. It may help Robby. It may even help me.

28

James's Journal
Tuesday, March 25th

I can hardly believe the events of today.

Things began much as usual, except that I had decided to drop my military title. I told Parkin first and asked him to instruct Henri and Antoine.

"Henri is not here today, sir."

"Then tell him tomorrow."

Parkin left a long silence, then said, "Very good, sir."

"You will tell them? The war is over, I have left the army, and there is no reason why anyone should continue to call me 'Colonel.'"

Another pause, as if he were waiting for me to change my mind. Finally he repeated, "Very good, sir."

Edmund came in while we were discussing it, if it could be called a discussion. Parkin can be infuriating. I know he is not in a position to argue with me, but he should not make his disagreement so plain unless he is prepared to say what he thinks.

Edmund merely looked puzzled when I told him. "You have been demobilised? But you have the right to keep your rank, do you not, since you were in the regular army?"

I threw up my arms in frustration. "I have not been demobilised. I was invalided out last year. I am a civilian now. It is not a question of rights. It is a question of . . . I do not need to explain. I am asking you — commanding you — to refer to me as 'Mr. Clarynton' in future."

Parkin and Edmund exchanged a glance, and Parkin said, "Very good, sir," for the third time.

I ignored him. "Vaughan, will you know what to do in letters and so on?"

"I think so. When I refer to you in the third person, I assume it will be The Honourable — you are keeping that? The Honourable J. B. V. Clarynton. And the VC?"

Parkin made a noise that I think was a guffaw disguised as a cough.

I ignored him and said to Edmund, "Yes. I certainly do not intend to insult the king by returning the Victoria Cross, and I will also keep the *Hon*. My father would strip me of it if he could, and therefore I shall continue to use it."

Why did they make such a fuss? I simply do not want Edmund to have to call me "Colonel" when he is living with his brother's disgrace. There is enough distance between us already. Besides, lieutenant colonel is a ridiculous rank for a man of my age. That and the crutches make me feel like a doddering dotard.

We settled down to work. I had read the book straight through on Sunday evening, and I suggested to Edmund that we should divide one chapter into two.

I say *we* as if there were two authors, and it is not far from the truth. His name must go inside, I thought as I gave him dictation. I must acknowledge his work in some way. Dare I dedicate it to him? *To E.V.I., without whom this book would never have been finished.* Or *To E.V.I., without whom the author would have lost his mind.* Or *To E.V.I., without whom the day would lose its sunlight and the night its stars.* I rather like the last one.

The morning passed . . . lunch . . . the early afternoon. I had no presentiment of any great event on the horizon.

At teatime Parkin said, "Mr. Vaughan has finished his work, sir, and shall he come in with it?"

"Yes. You can bring his tea in here. We'll have it together."

Edmund and the tea arrived at the same time. Rather to my surprise, he did not take his usual place at the dictation table but handed me the papers and sat in an armchair. Parkin put the tray on a low table between us, with the handle of the teapot facing Edmund.

I signed the letters and glanced at the revised chapters. "Splendid. I'll go through it properly tomorrow, unless there's anything in particular you want to discuss?"

"There is . . . although it's not about the work."

I looked at him more closely. There was something different about him—a stiffness, a determination, as if he faced some trial.

I leaned over to put the papers on the dictation table. "Would you mind pouring the tea? I have to ask everyone. I cannot manage it right-handed because of my shoulder, and I make an awful mess if I try to do it with the left."

"Of course." His knuckles were white as he poured first milk, then tea, filling both cups to precisely the same level.

I took a lump of sugar and stirred it into my tea. He did the same. I replaced my spoon while he continued to stir, gazing into his cup. He has not worn the dark glasses since his illness, and his long, dark lashes stood out against his pale skin.

He put his spoon down, placing it carefully in the saucer and straightening it with the tip of one finger. Finally, he raised his head.

Our eyes met. I let him see I had been watching him, and the two spots of colour appeared on his cheeks. He seemed so vulnerable without the glasses that my heart ached for him. I felt I was looking into his soul—a troubled, brave, and steadfast soul. If he had been under my command at the front, I would have trusted him to do his duty, whatever it cost.

He looked away first, and I broke the silence. "You wanted to speak to me?"

"Yes." He picked up his spoon again, clearly realised he had no use for it, and put it down. "There are things I must tell you. I have not been honest with you, but I am free to tell the truth, now my mother is—is gone."

I was tempted to wait, to see what he would say and what he would not, but I did not want to make this any harder for him than it had to be, so I spoke.

"Perhaps I can save you the trouble. Your name is Ingreham, is it not? Edmund Vaughan Ingreham?"

A flush crept over his cheeks. "Edmund Arthur Vaughan Ingreham. How long have you known?"

"Only since you were ill. I was anxious about you— very anxious. I wanted to find you, to know how you were. I did a little digging."

"Does Parkin know? Everybody?"

"I have not told anybody. Parkin may have guessed, but if he has, he hasn't said so. One friend of mine knows your name but nothing more."

"More?" He sat upright and combed his hair back with his hand.

"You are a grandson of the fourth earl of Akingbourne, are you not?"

He grimaced. "That is a generous way to describe my parentage."

"But it is true?"

"Yes."

"And you had an older brother who was convicted of desertion at court-martial last year."

He stared. "You know about Charles?"

"Yes. Why was he conscripted, when you were not? Or did he volunteer?"

"No, he was conscripted. Charles was born in Italy, not in Ireland, and he was working in London when conscription was introduced. He did not try to claim an exemption." Edmund sat forward in his chair. "But I do not understand. You knew about Charles, and you have not dismissed me. Aren't you angry?"

"Why? Because you concealed it from me? No, I see why you did that. And regarding your brother, he must have been unlucky." I had managed to convince myself of this.

"Unlucky?"

"Thousands of men were convicted of desertion. Very few of them were . . . executed." I had not wanted to use the word, but I could not find a better one. "In most cases, especially towards the end of the war, they were considered to have lost their reason under fire and were imprisoned."

Edmund looked down at his cooling tea. "I cannot defend what he did. He was not under fire but safely behind the lines, carrying orders to his company. He said he had lost his way back to their position, but he had stolen civilian clothes from a washing line and put them on, so he must have intended to flee. And to make matters worse, he had discarded the orders with his uniform. Anyone could have found them." The red patches on his cheeks deepened, and his voice took on a rough edge. "Men died because those orders did not get through."

This was harder to forgive. It caught me off-balance, and old angers constricted my chest. With difficulty, I brought myself back to the man sitting before me.

"All the same, it was not you who did this."

He frowned. "But you were a hero. You won the Victoria Cross. You would not have taken me on if you had known."

"Perhaps not, but that does not mean I will dismiss you now—now that I know your worth and have come to rely on you. You are not your brother, and I refuse to blame you for his crime, as you seem to wish me to do. I am sure you and he were not alike. You have an exceedingly strong character, though you hide it beneath a veneer of timidity."

My voice, I realised, had risen to the point where I sounded annoyed with him. I took another sip of tea, waiting for my emotion to subside.

When I was calm, I said, "While we are on the subject of your father, I should tell you I have also heard a certain amount of information—or gossip—about him and about your parents' marriage. None of it concerns me in relation to my employment of you. I remain entirely satisfied with you and your work."

"Thank you."

He did not move, so I said, "Do you have anything else to tell me?"

"No—or yes... I wanted to ask you something, but..." He picked up his cup, which was still full, and stared into it. After a long pause, he said, "I should like to explain a little more about my brother—I mean Robby—and what happened last year."

I sat back on the couch. He spoke with many hesitations, which I will not attempt to record here.

"Robby has tuberculosis, as you know. Last year our doctor in England recommended that he should go into a sanatorium for a rest and fresh air cure. My mother enquired into several places and settled on a famous one in Davos, in Switzerland. It is expensive, but with Charles in the army and me in Belfast, no longer dependent on her, my mother's income would have covered it. I took a leave of absence from my job to help her get him there. She gave up our house and sold our furniture, and we set off with Robby."

He stroked the teapot handle with two fingers. "We had reached France when we heard that Charles had been arrested. We stayed in an hotel in Paris and waited for the court-martial. My mother wanted him to have a lawyer, so she sent for one from England. It did not help, but it made us feel we were doing all we could for Charles." He came to himself and brought his hand away from the teapot. "More tea?"

"Thank you." I pushed my cup towards him, and he refilled it. He still had not tasted his.

"Between the hotel and the lawyer, we spent a great deal of money, but it did not seem to matter. However, when Charles — when Charles — "

He came to a stammering halt. I said gently, "Your mother's income stopped when the relation who was supporting her heard of your brother's conviction?"

"Yes." His head jerked up, and his expression clouded. "How did you know? Oh — Lady Diana Grantleigh?"

"Yes."

"She knows who I am?"

"No. I pretended an interest in the family at Akingbourne. It is another friend who knows your name, and I trust his discretion. Diana has left Paris, by the way, so you will not meet her again for some time."

He nodded, but this news did not appear to give him much relief. His gaze was on me now, but it was vacant, as if his thoughts were elsewhere.

I prompted him. "Your mother had spent a great deal of money and no longer had any coming in, so the three of you moved out of the hotel to rooms in Auteuil, and you began work at the American Red Cross under the name of Vaughan?"

"Yes. I had prolonged my leave of absence to the point where my employers in Belfast had engaged a replacement and did not want me back. And after our cousin cut off his support, I was afraid I would not find work in Paris under my real name. I feared others would have heard about

Charles's conviction, would share our cousin's disgust with us, and would not employ me."

"So you used your middle name?"

"It was Mama's suggestion, and it seemed to pay off. The Red Cross took me on at once. It was so easy, I thought I should have no difficulty in getting another post when they did not need me any more. I had not understood how much difference the armistice would make. It was much harder to find anything in the winter, and we had to dip into the money we had saved."

"I see. And what is the current situation? You have saved again since you have been working for me, but the money has gone on the medical expenses and the funeral?"

"A lot of it, yes, and the doctor says Robby must go to a sanatorium now. We cannot wait any longer." He swirled the cold tea around in his cup. "My mother thought a patient who has faith in his treatment has a better chance of getting well, so she encouraged Robby to believe that the place she had chosen was the best in the world for his case and was sure to cure him. Unfortunately, it is beyond my means."

A spasm crossed his face. "The doctor has told me of clinics in France, but the ones I can afford do not sound good at all. They are crowded, with very little treatment—really only rest homes where people are left to prevent them infecting others, like leper colonies. If he goes to a place like that, he will give up hope, and then he will not live long." He put his head in his hands. "I cannot bear to lose him too."

I longed to go to him, to comfort him, but feared my touch would only distress him more.

Finally he straightened up, took a deep breath, and rubbed his eyes.

"Perhaps I can help," I offered.

I thought he might ask for a salary increase, a loan, or both. I would have given them willingly. I did not expect what he said.

His eyes were wild, and the blood had drained out of his face. His hands clenched into fists as if he were drawing on all his courage.

"Yes. I wanted to ask you—if you have not replaced Louis Duquesne—if you might want me on the same terms?"

29

James's Journal, continued

I was filled with horror. I cannot now say why. Did I not long to have him for my own? But not like that... No, not like that. I would not buy his love.

My hand jerked involuntarily and knocked over my cup. Tea flooded the tray. Edmund glanced down at the mess, then pulled out a handkerchief and mopped at it.

I said, "I cannot accept your offer."

He let go of the handkerchief and stared at me. Desperation filled his eyes — the same expression I had seen in the library when I had teased him about the book. He twisted up out of his chair and took a step towards the door.

"No!" I leaned over and slammed the end of my crutch against the door, holding it closed. "Do not run from me. I cannot agree because it would kill something in you — and in me. But I have not finished. Hear me out. You shall have what you need. I will increase your salary."

He stood still, pale and tense. "It is already too generous."

"You deserve it. Your work is excellent."

But he shook his head. I did not need to ask why. His pride would not allow him to accept more money unless he earned it.

An idea came to me. "When your brother is in Switzerland, you will not need to keep your lodgings. You can move in here, as my permanent secretary. There are two spare bedrooms in the apartment. You may choose whichever you prefer. I shall be taking a great deal more of your time that way, so of course I shall pay you ... let us say twice what you earn now, and you will not have the cost of a room and board. Will that be enough?"

He ran a hand through his hair. "I think it would, but I do not know if I can take it."

He would have prostituted himself, but he would not accept a higher salary!

"It is for Robert, not for you," I said. "If the boy has a better chance in Switzerland, in the clinic your mother chose, then that is where he must go."

A light came into his eyes. Then it died, and he shook his head again. "It will only make it harder when he has to leave."

"Why should he have to leave?"

"You will soon finish your book."

"I shall still need you. By then I will be more mobile, if all goes well. I will be able to escape my doctors and take a house outside Paris, or travel, perhaps. There will be a great deal to do—correspondence to write, arrangements to make..." I waved a hand as if to indicate tasks too numerous to list. "It is common, is it not, for a wealthy man to have a resident secretary?"

"Is it? I do not know."

"It is," I said firmly—although when I reflect on this now, I realise it is only those wealthy men who spend their time on politics, business, or authorship who employ a secretary in this way. Well, I cannot go into politics in France, but I can write another book or invest in a business, if I must.

I lowered the crutch. I had wrenched my shoulder in preventing him from leaving the room, and it hurt abominably. "Think about it if you like, and we can discuss it another time."

"Thank you. Yes, I must think." He looked down at the tray. "Should I—"

"If you would be kind enough to ring for Parkin as you go, he will take care of it."

He rang and left the room, stopping in the doorway to thank me once again in an abstracted way.

When Parkin came, I said, "I have spilled some tea."

"Yes, sir." He bent to pick up the tray, on which lay Edmund's handkerchief. I was seized with a foolish desire to take it and keep it, tea-stained as it was, to remind me of this day and the offer he had made.

But I let it lie and only added, "And I have hurt my shoulder. Telephone the man and ask him to come now, will you?"

Parkin came back a few minutes later to tell me the shoulder man was visiting a client outside Paris and would not return until tomorrow.

"Damn. I suppose you couldn't—no." Parkin's hands are not strong. He tore something in an accident involving a billiard ball many years ago, and he has to take care. "Henri?"

"It is Tuesday, sir"—Henri's day off—"and I think Antoine is out. Perhaps Mr. Vaughan might help you?"

"Has he not gone home?"

"I believe he is still in the library."

I glanced at the clock. It was not yet six. "I would rather not summon him again. He is under some stress at the moment, and I can wait for Antoine."

"Very good, sir." Parkin opened the door, carrying the tray, but instead of passing through, he stood back and held it open. Edmund was there, looking haunted.

He came to the dictation table and stood with his hands resting on the back of the chair. When the door had closed behind Parkin, I said, "Well? Have you thought?" Pain made me irritable.

"Yes. I shall accept, for Robby's sake."

My heart leaped, and joy wiped out the pain—but only for a moment.

"Good," I grunted. "Now, can you do something for my shoulder? I have thrown it out. You need to get behind me and manipulate it." He came around the couch and took hold of my shoulder with hesitant hands.

"Yes, there, but harder."

He took me at my word. His hands were stronger than I would have thought possible. My shoulder was trapped in an iron vice. The pain lashed me with tongues of fire, and I swore.

He relaxed his hold. "Have I hurt you?"

"Don't stop, damn it! You *must* hurt me. That is the point."

He gripped my shoulder again and pushed—and the thing went right.

"That's it. Stop now!"

He took his hands away. The pain was gone.

I wiped perspiration from my forehead with the back of my other hand. "There is an example of your new duties."

He moved around to stand in front of me. He was smiling. I believe I smiled back.

"Well, go on," I said. "Get off home and give Robert the news. I expect you'll want to start making arrangements to travel, won't you?"

"Yes, thank you." He was radiant now. I had my own private sun in the salon. "When would it be convenient for me to go?"

"Whenever you like. How long will you need to be away? Will two weeks be enough?"

"It might, but it is Robby's birthday on the fifteenth of April. I should not like to leave him before that."

I told him to stay as long as necessary, and then I let him go. It will take him several days to make the arrangements, so I will see him again before they leave. Then I shall be a mass of impatience, waiting for his return.

If I had accepted his offer, he might have been with me now, here in my bed. Was it madness to refuse? How will it be, to have him living with me and not be able to touch?

Living with me — that is the thing.

My cheeks ache from smiling.

30

Edmund's Journal
Tuesday, March 25th

He does not want me—or he does not want me for his kept man.

What does he want? I am not sure. Nor am I sure how I feel. I was humiliated when he said no, but only for a moment. He made all well very quickly, somehow.

I long to touch him again. My hands still feel the firm warmth of his shoulder. I wanted to kiss it, to caress it, instead of manipulating it. But I think he is right. What I proposed would have been bad for us both. His plan may be better.

I will take Robby to Switzerland and come back... and then we shall see.

31

James's Journal
Tuesday, April 1st

They have gone.

Edmund brought his things here on the way to the station. He has so little—one bag, which he has not unpacked, except to take out a photograph of his mother. Their trunk is going with Robert, but I doubt there is much more in that.

I went down to the street to see them off. I wanted to accompany them to the station, but I would only have been a nuisance, holding them up, so I sent Parkin with them. He will find them good seats and make sure they have all they need.

Robert said goodbye to me with shining eyes, eager to be away on his big adventure. Edmund had a worry line between his brows. I am sorry they must be separated— Edmund will feel it—but I cannot help being glad that I shall have Edmund to myself.

By the time I came back up, alone, the cab had gone and the street below was empty.

Edmund has chosen the smaller of the two spare rooms, the one with the less interesting view. He would not have been successful in Louis's circle. He does not have the instinct that makes those men grasp at every advantage.

*

I said nothing to Edmund before he left, but I have been thinking that the arrangement I proposed does not offer them enough security. It makes Edmund too dependent on me.

What if he wanted to leave my employment? There cannot be many posts that pay so well, and he might be forced to stay with me for Robert's sake. Such an obligation could cause resentment from the start—resentment against me, since his natural feelings would not allow him to direct it at Robert.

Of course, I do not want him to look for other work, but nor do I want to bind him to me with ties that may irritate. I want him to *choose* to stay.

I shall discuss it with Finlayson, the lawyer, while Edmund is away.

Thursday, April 3rd

They should be in Switzerland now. When will they reach Davos? I see from the atlas that it is on the eastern side of the country, high in the mountains. It must be an interesting and beautiful journey. I wish I had asked for their itinerary. I should like to be able to think *Now they are at A* and *Now they are at B*.

Edmund promised to send me his address when they arrived. When can I expect to hear? Sunday or Monday, perhaps? Or will he be too busy to write at once?

A letter from Diana. The banns are read and she is to be married at St. Margaret's, Westminster, next week.

By the way, she writes, *Mummy tells me they heard at Akingbourne that Lady Elizabeth Ingreham died of influenza some weeks ago — in Paris! Had you met her? Is that why you asked about her? Do tell me everything. I should have adored knowing someone so deliciously scandalous, and knowing someone who knew her would be the next best thing.*

From the little Edmund has said of his mother, and from the photograph that now stands beside his bed, I fear she would have been a disappointment to Diana. She appears to have been a quiet, well-mannered lady in faded middle age. In any case, I can reply quite truthfully that I never met her, although I had heard that she had died.

32

Letter, Edmund to James
Davos, Sunday, April 6th

Dear Mr. Clarynton,

We have arrived safely, and I have taken a room in a small boardinghouse to which you can write if you have any instructions for me—in the name of Ingreham, of course.

The mountains are breathtaking, covered with the purest white snow, though the sky above is blue and the sunlight strong. The air is so clean, it is a delight to fill one's lungs. We have arrived just before the changing of the seasons, with snow still falling from time to time but soon to thaw here in the high valley. They tell us that the slopes around us will then burst into blossom with a carpet of spring flowers, some of which grow nowhere else in the world.

Robert is happily installed at the sanatorium. The journey tired him, but a day or two of rest in this air has put him right. The doctors inspire confidence, and the nursing staff are kind. In the next bed is an Italian boy close to his own age with whom he has made friends, although they can only converse in broken French.

If convenient to you, I shall stay until after his birthday and arrive back in Paris on, I think, the twentieth.

I thank you once again for your generosity in giving my brother this opportunity.

Your servant,

E. A. Vaughan Ingreham

Letter, James to Edmund
Paris, Friday, April 11th

my dear vaughan (or ingreham),

i have no instructions for you, but i cannot resist the impulse to show you that your typewriter is not idle in your absence.

the man entrusted with the care of my shoulder tells me that when you manipulated it, you put it more right than it has ever been, and it must now be allowed to set in this position. my arm is therefore in a sling, and i am forbidden to use it. i must get about on one crutch or in a wheeled chair. i cannot write with the left hand well enough for anyone's eyes but my own, but i am able to pick out words with the oddly arranged keys of your machine, except for the capital letters, which i cannot find.

i never needed a secretary more than i do now, but in your much-regretted absence i am grateful to have this mechanical substitute.

i hear that everyone who goes to switzerland returns with a cuckoo clock. i trust you will be the exception. if you do take a fancy to such a thing, be warned it must inhabit your own room, unless you can charm parkin and henri into accepting it beyond the baize door.

those two gentlemen await your return almost as eagerly as
 your friend,
 james clarynton

James's Journal
Sunday, April 13th

Dreadful left-handed scrawl, but it is for myself alone.

Last night I went to a supper party with Claude. As we left, he found he had forgotten his scarf and went back inside, leaving me on the street in the wheeled chair. Three young men passed me, talking excitedly. One of them turned and came back to me. It was Loulou.

He regarded my chair and sling with concern and began to tell a long story of a friend who smashed an elbow in a skating accident. His gestures were so wild and his voice so loud that I wondered if he was drunk. However, there was no smell of alcohol on his breath.

He wanted to take me to a house where one can get anything one wants in the range of men and boys for a price. My disabilities would be no barrier, he said. He grasped the handles of my chair.

I had to say, "No, Louis, do not push me away. I am waiting for a friend."

"The secretary with the handsome eyes?"

"No, he has gone out of France."

Fortunately Claude had set the brake and Louis did not see how to release it, or he would have carried me off.

One is powerless when confined to those chairs. I understand why Robert longed for crutches instead.

Claude emerged at last, and I said a hasty goodbye to Louis. He greeted Claude coldly and did not detain or follow us, to my relief.

"I believe he is taking something," I said to Claude when we were clear of him.

"Yes, cocaine. It is too expensive for him. He has become desperate, and it is no longer possible to introduce him to anybody. Do not be tempted to take up with him again, *mon cher*, even briefly."

"I shall not." I felt uneasy, all the same. "I hope it was nothing I did that set him on this path."

Claude laughed. "No, do not think yourself so important. He began to take it in the war, they tell me, and his appetite was certain to outgrow his income sooner or later."

He dismissed the matter and talked of other things, but I could not put Loulou out of my mind so quickly. I feel I let him down, although I do not see what else I could have done — I was not the first man to buy the services he offered, and I will not be the last.

Letter, Edmund to James
Davos, Wednesday, April 16th

Dear Mr. Clarynton,

I cannot thank you enough for your kindness to Robby. He has written to you himself, enclosed herewith and sealed — I was not permitted to read it — but I must add my own note of gratitude.

Yesterday morning was a happy time, as he opened his presents from me and enjoyed the good wishes of staff and patients, followed by a special cake. Later, however, our thoughts went to his last birthday and the sad changes in our family since then, and we both became rather low and dull.

Then your parcel arrived so unexpectedly, and I cannot tell you what a difference it made. The unwrapping was a great excitement, and he remained bright and cheerful for the rest of the day. He was delighted with your gifts and even happier, I think, to know there is someone in the world thinking of him, besides me — since we have not heard from our father for some years, and Robby has no memory of him.

I leave here tomorrow and shall be in Paris on Sunday, if all runs to time.

Yours with sincere thanks once again,

E. A. Vaughan Ingreham

P.S. In case you have not already discovered it, to type capital letters with one hand you must first engage the Shift Lock. Type the required letter, then press the lower Shift key to release the lock.

P.P.S. I have resisted all pressure to buy a cuckoo clock so far, but the Swiss are most insistent, and I fear it may be illegal to leave the country without one.

Letter, Robert Ingreham to James Clarynton
Davos, Wednesday, April 16th

Dear Mr. Clarynton,

Thank you so much for the two books and the jigsaw puzzle. Before your parcel arrived, I thought I had had everything and nothing else would happen, so it was the most terrific surprise.

I am saving the books until Edmund has gone, but I looked inside them and they both seem awfully good. Edmund read the first page of *The Adventures of Sherlock Holmes* and thought it might be too mature for someone of twelve, but I am sure he is wrong. Luckily he agreed that as you chose it for me, I should be allowed to keep it.

Jules Verne is French, isn't he? I am glad you sent the English translation of *Around the World in Eighty Days*. I do not think I could have read it in the original language. Edmund says I must improve my French if I want to talk to anybody here, but that is not true. I manage very well. Besides, some of the doctors and patients speak English, and the local people do not speak French at all, but a special kind of German.

I have set up the jigsaw map of Paris in the room where we go when we are allowed out of bed. Everyone has helped with it. Many of the gentlemen are familiar with the city, and it has led to some lively discussions — mostly in French, however. I believe I should have discovered a great deal about Life if I could have followed them better. Perhaps I would benefit from improving my French, after all.

I am glad that Edmund will live with you in Paris. I should not like to think of him living alone. He is often troubled and needs cheering up. I am sure you and Mr. Parkin will cheer him up admirably.

I expect that is impertinent, so I must stick down my envelope before Edmund comes. I hope your wounds are not troubling you excessively just now. Are they better in dry weather, like my chest?

Yours sincerely,
R. J. V. Ingreham

Edmund's Journal
Switzerland, Friday, April 18th

I am on my way home—to Paris, I mean.

The return timetable requires me to break my journey in different places, so I slept last night in a town I had not visited with Robby. It was strange to have no one with whom to share my impressions of the place.

I continue towards the French border today. The trains spiral around the mountains, crossing viaducts and puffing through tunnels. The distances are much greater than they appear on a map because of the roundabout routes we must take.

The Swiss are attractive people, combining strict adherence to rules and regulations with a charming pastoral simplicity. Goats are kept more often than sheep in the mountains, and when the train stops at a country station, one may catch the tinkle of cowbells. At Davos, when I went walking out of the town, I often heard a goatherd yodelling to his flock. Yet they do not seem backward or dreamy, but practical and businesslike.

I spent some time at my last stop searching for a present for my employer. I could not think what to give him, since I am sure he buys himself all that he wants. The Swiss are known for their clock-making, but he wears a watch on his wrist that works perfectly well, and after his comments about cuckoo clocks, I did not want to get anything similar. In the end I chose a cowbell — a token gift, almost a joke, which he can use to summon me if he wishes or bury in a cupboard if not.

Before I left Davos, I said to Robby, "You might mention Mr. Clarynton in your prayers, when you think of it. He has helped us a great deal."

He turned to me with an eager face. "But I do, always — ever since we went in his carriage."

"That is kind of you. Do you ask God to take away his pain?"

"No. I don't think he minds about the pain, not really. I ask God to make him happy."

I wonder if he asks the same for me. What would he think if James and I found that happiness together?

33

James's Journal
Sunday, April 20th

Edmund returned this afternoon. There is sunlight in the apartment again.

I did not hear his knock. I had persuaded myself he would come sooner if I did not spend every moment watching and listening for him. When he came into the salon, bright-eyed and smiling, I was so surprised that I cried out, "Edmund! You are home!"

He stopped short. I recovered myself and added, "You must forgive my using your first name. I do not know which of your other names to use."

His smile returned. "Ingreham, I think, if it will not embarrass you."

"Not at all." I reached for my crutch and hoisted myself up. "You are looking well. The mountain air must have agreed with you."

"Yes, and it gave me an appetite." He patted his stomach. The extra pounds suit him. He was painfully thin when he left.

"Excellent. You will dine with me? You may still have your lunch hours to yourself if you wish, but I trust you will have dinner with me each evening. Parkin could hardly serve us both a full meal at the same time in two different places, and the secretary dines with the family in all the best houses."

Is this true? I think so. My father never employed a secretary, but I met one or two while visiting friends. In any case, the food would have stuck in my throat if I'd had to eat alone that evening while Edmund dined in the library.

He hesitated, but he must have believed me — or perhaps he only wanted to save Parkin extra work. He said, "Thank you. I shall go and change."

When he had gone, I rang for Parkin and said, "Mr. Vaughan will now be known as Mr. Ingreham, which is, in fact, his name."

"Very good, sir." Parkin's face was inscrutable. Had he guessed, I wonder, after our conversation about Captain Ingreham and the elopement? He did not look surprised, but then he never does.

"And he will dine with me, this evening and every evening."

"Yes, sir." He said this with no hint of the disapproval he showed over serving us lunch together. I must have been right about dining customs in the best houses.

"Might you have time to find some flowers for the table?" I asked.

"I have already seen to it."

"You are a miracle, Parkin."

"Yes, sir" — with a bow, and the slightest of smiles.

Flowers, candlelight, and plate after plate of Henri's specialities. No need to tempt Edmund's appetite now. He tucked in to every dish. He talked more than I have ever heard him too, about Robert, about Switzerland, about his journey home. For me, it combined into one soothing song—*Edmund is here.*

He excused himself immediately after dinner, saying he was tired and wanted to write to Robert. I was reluctant to let him go, but I must be patient and not devour him. He is as skittish as a fawn.

It is wonderful to have him living here. I cannot quite believe it. I tread very carefully to avoid frightening him away. He has looked at me once or twice as if he expects something from me, but everything must be in place before I make another move. I cannot yet enjoy his company completely. I feel as I did when planning to advance on the front line—that success will require great care because one must not only arrive at the new position, but also hold it.

Now that he no longer wears his glasses, I find myself watching his long-lashed eyes all the time. They are so expressive! Every thought and mood seems to pass through them. I have seen joy, sadness, concern, and even, I think, a flash of desire—but I might have imagined that.

I must be certain. I do not want him to come to me from mere gratitude.

Tuesday, April 22nd

Finlayson arrived from London yesterday with the papers, and I had a short meeting with him alone today. He was my uncle's lawyer, and I trust him absolutely.

I consulted him about Louis, preferring to do this in person than by letter, although it will mean Finlayson staying longer. His advice was to make a final payment dependent upon Louis signing an agreement not to contact me again, but I do not want to give him any more money to spend on the drug. After some discussion, we agreed that Finlayson will purchase a few years' lease on a small coastal villa where Louis can escape the temptations of Paris, as I believe part of him must wish to do. If I am wrong, he may resell the lease at once, but I shall have given him a chance.

Regarding Edmund, Finlayson has done everything exactly as I wished. He made no comment about the Ingreham name, though it was clear from our conversation that he knew about the scandal of twenty-five years ago. Nor did he seek any explanation from me of the settlement I have made. He only stipulated that Edmund should sign a waiver, like Louis. I would have preferred to avoid this, not wanting to act as if the two cases were similar in any way, but he insisted.

I did not give Finlayson an appointment here for the signing lest the transaction haunt our domestic life, so we shall meet in a private room at his hotel tomorrow. When I told Edmund about it, he seemed surprised that I wished him to be there.

"It concerns you," I said. "It will regularise our arrangement."

He frowned a little, as if he thought that unnecessary. I said no more. I would prefer Finlayson to explain it, to avoid any misunderstanding.

Later

I had ordered a posy for Edmund's room to welcome him home. I did not want to overwhelm him with scent or variety, so I chose peonies, three burgundy globes in a mass of foliage.

He had not mentioned them, so this evening I asked Parkin, "Do you think he has noticed the flowers?"

"Oh yes, sir, he has moved them from the dressing table and placed them beside his bed."

My heart leaped, but then I thought to ask, "Which side? The side with the photograph or the other?"

"He has put them next to the photograph," Parkin said.

So he has given my flowers to his mother. Ah well, they are his to use however he wishes . . . as everything I give him will be.

Wednesday, April 23rd

The sling is off at last. Edmund still wanted to take me to Finlayson's hotel in the wheeled chair, but I refused. It would put me in the same category as his brother — someone who is dependent on him, someone he looks after. I did not want to be in that position.

Perhaps the meeting would have gone more smoothly if I had allowed it.

We arrived before the time. The room was ready for us, but we did not sit down at once. Edmund might have, I think, but I was restless, and he will not sit if I am standing. He defers to me as a secretary should, and I am only now beginning to wish he would not. But we are not yet at that point of equality.

Finlayson bustled in with the papers, and I introduced Edmund. They shook hands. Finlayson sat at the end of the table, while Edmund and I faced each other on either side.

Finlayson turned to Edmund. "Well now, Mr. Clarynton has no doubt told you—"

"I have told him nothing," I cut in.

"Ah." Finlayson raised one eyebrow. "Then, Mr. Ingreham, Mr. Clarynton has settled on you a sum of money, with the intention, I believe, that you will live on the quarterly interest."

"It will bring you the amount we discussed," I said.

Edmund's brows drew together. "What amount?"

"The salary we agreed before you went away."

"But what does he mean about it being settled on me?"

With a gesture I indicated that Finlayson should answer.

"Mr. Clarynton transferred to my firm's client account an amount of capital that I have invested in bonds on your behalf." Finlayson passed a document to Edmund. "It will pay you an income, but the whole sum is in your name. This waiver specifies the amount. If you accept the settlement, I should be grateful if you would be so good as to sign it."

Edmund took the paper. As his eyes moved down it, his body grew still and his face paled. The room became so quiet that Finlayson's breathing sounded like a gale.

"I cannot accept this."

Finlayson now raised both eyebrows. "You do not consider it to be enough?"

"I consider it to be far too much." The familiar spots of colour appeared on Edmund's cheeks, and he met my gaze with a look of incomprehension. "We agreed you would pay me a salary."

"The result is the same," I said. "You will have the same income, but with more security. I do not want you and Robert to be in the same position as your mother, where your income could cease at any moment on a whim of mine. My first thought was to give you a contract of employment guaranteeing payment for a certain number of years, but Finlayson pointed out that such a contract could be challenged if I died during its term. I cannot solve that with a legacy because my family would contest it. My father and brother are so disgusted with my—my way of life, let us say, that I am sure they would not allow any male friend of mine to benefit after my death without a fight. They would drag you through a court case that could do untold damage to your reputation, unless you gave up any claims on my estate. So we required another solution. Finlayson suggested a trust, but I do not believe we need anything so complicated."

Edmund opened his mouth to speak, then closed it again.

I gestured to the document. "This is what we have arranged. The invested sum is yours now, unconditionally. If I were to die tonight, it would not be part of my estate, and your right to it would be clear. If you were to die, I assume it would go to Robert."

Finlayson coughed. "Such assumptions are unsafe and, in this case, unlikely to be correct. I strongly advise you to make a will, Mr. Ingreham."

I rapped my fingers on the table, annoyed with myself. "Yes, I forgot your father is alive. He would get it. You should certainly make a will."

"But this is . . ." Edmund looked down at the paper. "This represents some twenty-five years at the salary you offered. It is good of you, but I cannot accept. It would put me under an obligation for too long."

I sat back and folded my arms. "Nonsense. There is no obligation."

"Your signature on the document will not commit you to anything but accepting the transfer in full and final settlement," Finlayson added.

Edmund's brows set in a stubborn line as he turned to me. "Not legally, perhaps, but in my mind I would feel bound to you for all of those twenty-five years. What if I wished to leave your service? I could not do it with a clear conscience. You are trying to buy me as an indentured servant."

"I am doing no such thing!" Heat rushed to my head. I stamped my crutch on the floor. "That is most unfair, when just one month ago—"

I stopped speaking because I did not want Finlayson to know that Edmund had offered to sell himself to me that day, but I glared at Edmund, and he obviously understood me. His cheeks turned a deeper shade of red.

Finlayson put a restraining hand on my arm. "Mr. Clarynton, please. If I might explain it to him . . ."

I jerked my arm away. "Certainly you may explain it. That is why we are here!"

He turned to Edmund and said in soothing tones, "Mr. Ingreham, this gift is entirely without obligation, either legal or moral. The income from it will be five percent per annum, which Mr. Clarynton believes will be enough to provide you with the necessities of life and to support your brother in his sanatorium. If this is the case, you need not draw on the capital. You could, if you wished, return all or part of it at any time, by making over the bonds or a proportion of them to Mr. Clarynton."

Edmund's stiff shoulders relaxed a little. "You mean my brother and I could live on the interest, so the original sum would remain intact, and I could simply give it back if I wished to leave Mr. Clarynton's service?"

"Yes. Your own lawyer would advise you not to do that, however, because your income—your means of supporting your brother—would then cease with immediate effect."

I broke in, "This is not a loan. It is a gift. My uncle left me extremely well off. I spend only a small part of my income, and I will not miss what I am giving you. I want to provide you and Robert with security. If you leave me, I expect you to keep every penny. However, if that felt unbearable to you, you could give some of it back or put it in trust for Robert or dispose of it however you wished. It is yours."

Edmund bit his lip—a sight that stirred my blood.

I added, "I have not done this to put you under an obligation. Quite the opposite. I have done it to make you independent of me. I do not want to have to pay you a salary each week or each month. I want there to be no question of money between us."

He frowned. "But then I would not have to be your secretary at all."

"No. I hope you enjoy the work enough to continue with it, but you do not have to. Nor do you have to live in my apartment—but do not forget it would cost you something to live elsewhere."

His brow was still furrowed. "This is all very strange. May I think about it before I decide?" He stood and took the document to the window. "What does it mean by 'in full and final settlement'? You used the phrase just now, I think, Mr. Finlayson. In settlement of what?"

"Of any claim you may have on Mr. Clarynton."

"For your secretarial services," I put in hastily.

"For all services." But Finlayson nodded as he said this, as if he were agreeing with me rather than implying something very different. "In short, if you sign it, you will have undertaken not to ask Mr. Clarynton for anything more."

Edmund gave a short laugh. "Ask for *more*? Of course I will not."

"I do not care whether you sign it," I said. "It was Finlayson's idea."

"It is customary, in the circumstances," the lawyer murmured. I do not know what he thought the circumstances were, since I had told him Edmund was not to be regarded as a successor to Loulou.

After some minutes, Edmund came back to the table. He did not look at me as he said, "I think you are right, and this will allow me to support my brother without touching the capital. Therefore, I will accept. Thank you." He sat and signed.

He did not seem as happy as I had hoped. Have I misjudged him? Does he feel insulted?

34

Edmund's Journal
Thursday, April 24th

No journal yesterday because I wrote to Robby. I have promised to write twice a week, and he will do the same when he is strong enough. It means our letters will cross, but I will write every Wednesday and Sunday without fail.

I told James of this plan, adding, "The only disadvantage of such regularity is that he will worry if a letter is a day late."

James said, "I do not know your brother well, but I do not believe he worries as you do."

He is right, of course. How does he know, from his short acquaintance with Robby?

I said, "All the same, if I were ill . . ."

"If you were ill, I would write on your behalf."

This reassured me. If the past twelve months have taught me anything, it is that life is fragile. But James will make sure that Robby knows if something happens to me.

I am making a will, as Mr. Finlayson suggested. I had assumed it would be simple because I want everything to go to Robby, but it seems there must be a trust because of Robby's age, so I had to think of trustees. I chose James and Mr. Finlayson, and they advised me to have a third. I thought of my mother's lawyer in London, but James said lawyers charge fees for administering trusts. One lawyer is useful, but two are unnecessary and might eat up a significant amount of the income. Therefore I have named the headmaster of our old school. He may refuse to act, but it is only in case of my death before Robby is twenty-one, and soon perhaps I shall have made some other responsible friend who can take his place.

"You are now a man of independent means," James said to me in the carriage as we returned from the meeting with Mr. Finlayson yesterday.

I do not know what to say about that meeting. It still astonishes me. I have taken my copy of the document from my drawer three times today, to make sure it is true.

In brief, James has settled a large sum on me, which is mine outright. He has given me an investment that produces a private income. At five percent, it will be a little more than the huge salary I agreed with James before I left—almost as much as Mama used to have from our cousin for the comfortable maintenance of our family of four. I did not want to accept it at first, but I felt I must because it provides security for Robby.

Mr. Finlayson asked for the name of my bankers. He will arrange for the income to be paid to my account. He said there would be an amount immediately.

"What is this first payment?" I asked James on the way home. "Do not tell me it is the interest. I cannot believe it would be due so soon. And I do not need money now. You gave me an advance before I left for Switzerland, and the sanatorium fees are paid for this quarter."

"At the risk of irritating you, I hope you will use some of it to add to your wardrobe."

I did not like this. "I have told you I do not want to go to your tailor."

He put up his hands as if to ward off blows, making me laugh, despite my annoyance. "You do not have to. You may find one of your own—and you are not obliged to do that, if the suggestion offends you. Your suit is adequate for your work. But I hope you will sometimes accompany me when I go out, and you cannot always wear the same thing. You have good taste, but the trousers, in particular, are beginning to show their age."

He is right, and I shall do as he asks.

Independence has many advantages. I will always be indebted to James but I will not be newly indebted every week, as I was when my salary was paid. I shall try to please him, but I do not have to. I may say what I think. I need not take his requests as commands. I do not have to avoid angering him for fear of losing my post.

I am here because I want to be. I could live anywhere. I do not even have to work for him, although I am sure I will always want to. And best of all, when my will is signed, I will know that Robby will be able to stay at the sanatorium until he is well, no matter what happens to me.

What a weight this takes from my shoulders!

Pride still made me want to refuse James's charity, until I remembered that Mama was never proud. She accepted help from Lord Akingbourne year after year for our sakes, even though he would not acknowledge her in public and his wife would not meet her at all. James's gift does not come with insults.

But why did he give me such freedom?

35

James's Journal
Friday, April 25th

I shall have to tread carefully. Edmund is not proving as easy to win as I hoped. I wanted to take him to a recital this evening at Madame de Treguille's, but he did not leap at the chance.

"I have nothing to wear yet."

"That suit will do."

His face set into stubbornness — an expression I am coming to know well. "I will go in the carriage to help you in and out, if you like, but I will not stay. You were right about my clothes. I am not equipped to go into society."

He has found a tailor, but since it is not my own, I cannot insist on the man putting everything else aside and working day and night.

"You can wear something of mine," I said.

"It would be a poor fit." He has filled out a little, but I am still a broader man than he. "And how would you introduce me?"

"As my secretary," I growled.

"Will they not think it strange, when I have no invitation? You have never taken me anywhere before."

We continued like this for ten minutes before I abandoned the plan, admitting—to myself, not to him—that he was right.

I set off in a black mood, having rejected his offer to accompany me in the carriage.

Had I been paying him a salary, I could have demanded his presence at my side throughout the evening. He would have made no objection. But then I would never have known if he truly enjoyed the recital or was only saying so to be polite.

I will not compel him to share my social life. After all, I have more of his time than if he lived elsewhere and came daily. He dines with me every evening and breakfasts with me too, if I am careful to rise at the same hour. But he insists on the separate lunch that Parkin first recommended, and if I do not want to dictate to him in the morning, he goes for a solitary walk through the streets or sits in the park, enjoying the sights and sounds of Paris by himself.

I settled a sum on Edmund because I wanted him to be with me of his own free will. I cannot object if that is not what he chooses. And even if he feels nothing for me, I have done something good for Robert.

The music soothed me, and I have come home happier. I should have been happier still if Edmund had waited up for me, but he has not.

Well, the settlement is made, for better or worse. I must take it step by step, the taming of this gazelle.

36

Edmund's Journal
Friday, April 25th

I do not understand him. He does not touch me or invite his friends to meet me, but he expects to take me into society without invitation or suitable dress, as if I were one of those lapdogs that certain ladies take everywhere. Is that how he sees me — as a pet?

37

James's Journal
Tuesday, April 29th

Edmund continues to assert his independence.

I breakfasted alone this morning, assuming he was still asleep. At nine o'clock I swung through the apartment on my crutches in search of him. We have maintained the habit of dictation on Tuesday, Thursday, and Saturday mornings, and to my surprise we have almost reached the end of the second draft. It will still require some revision, of course, but we may achieve something publishable.

I knocked on the door of Edmund's room. He was not there. I had already looked in the salon and the library, so I went to find Parkin. "Where is he?"

"Mr. Ingreham rose early and has gone for a final fitting at his tailor's, sir. He said he would be back by ten o'clock."

Irritation prickled at my nerves. "He might have told me. I wanted to start early today."

Why had he said nothing the night before? Could it be that he wished the suit to be a surprise? No, he would have asked Parkin not to tell me, in that case.

I thought of opening my heart to Parkin and asking his advice, but I should have had to tell him of Edmund's offer, and I must not do that.

Instead, I turned to the piano.

The shoulder man was right about the sling. That and Edmund's ministrations have made all the difference. Even at this first attempt, I was able to play.

I went on longer than I should have, until my shoulder began to burn a little. Then I stopped and looked up. Edmund stood in the doorway.

"You play beautifully." Something in his eyes told me he was truly moved.

I dismissed his praise with a gesture. "I am out of practice, with the war and my injuries."

He came further into the room. "Did you learn at home?"

"Yes, I began there when I was quite small. We had a tutor who played a little, and my mother asked him to teach me. Then I went away to school, where I was lucky enough to find a good teacher. Music was an escape for me in the years after my mother died."

Edmund would understand that grief. I added, "Looking back, I am surprised my father allowed me to take music lessons, but he might have paid the bills without reading them. He did not like my playing at home. He thought it unmanly. In the school holidays, I had to practise when they were out hunting."

Edmund came closer still, leaning against the back of a chair. "You did not like blood sports?"

"I went shooting, but not foxhunting if I could avoid it. Being in the midst of a pack of bloodthirsty men and dogs, chasing one terrified creature for mile after mile, to tear it apart at the end—it turned my stomach. I always hoped the fox would go to ground."

Edmund nodded. His eyes were upon me, soft and steady, as if he wished to see into my soul.

I took advantage of the moment. "I hear you will soon be kitted out in apparel fitting your station. Would you care to accompany me to the opera on Saturday evening?"

He reddened at once. "I—"

"You will enjoy it, I am sure, and you cannot have any excuse. You will not need an invitation, only a ticket, and I have one to spare."

A smile teased the corners of his mouth. "Very well."

So that is settled. We shall see Nadia Rossakova in *Aïda*. I must be sure to pay enough attention to the performance to have something to say about it afterwards. With Edmund by my side, I may have trouble thinking of anything but him.

38

Edmund's Journal
Thursday, May 1st

My new clothes are here. I have never had anything that fit so well, and I take pleasure in walking around the apartment in them. They are so fine, I do not believe I shall ever put on that old suit again, unless it is to visit Mme. H. and our old neighbours in Auteuil. If I went there dressed as a prosperous gentleman, they might suspect some criminal enterprise!

James's eye lingers upon me whenever we meet. I feel powerful one moment and fragile the next, as if I might break him or be broken against him, and I cannot tell which. When he is with me, everything comes alive.

I was so lonely after Mama died, but sometimes now—it is terrible to confess—I am glad to be alone. I still miss her every hour and yearn to have her back, but that cannot be, and I choose to believe she would want me to be happy.

I never thought I would marry, so I always imagined my mother and brothers would be the limit of my existence. Now Mama and Charles are gone, and Robby is too far away to be affected by anything I do. Possibilities open before me like stepping stones to a magical shore.

I have accepted James's invitation to the opera. We go on Saturday night.

39

James's Journal
Sunday, May 4th, early hours

I cannot sleep. My heart is too full—full of joy beyond anything I had imagined. It lights my whole being, outshining the lamp that burns beside my bed as I sit up with this book.

I dressed for the opera early, paying more attention to my appearance than I have since I was wounded. I made Parkin brush my coat twice and scolded him for his liberality with the hair oil. In the end I was satisfied. The black patch and the foreshortened leg were as obvious as ever, but perhaps they are not as displeasing to the eye as I had assumed.

I straightened up and pulled back my shoulders in front of the glass. "Well, Parkin, you have succeeded in making me look—how shall I put it?—*distinguished* is the word, I think."

"Yes, sir," he said, accepting all the credit with a little smile. No false modesty there!

I sent him to help Edmund while I waited, fizzing with impatience, in the salon.

When Edmund joined me, he took my breath away. He was well-dressed, of course—that did not surprise me — but there was something new in his eyes. They glowed with happiness.

Most men would not allow such enthusiasm to show. It is fashionable to be cynical. But cynicism is foreign to Edmund, and I hope with all my heart it always will be.

"I don't suppose you have often been to the opera," I ventured as we waited for the lift. I did not dare to think his excitement might have been inspired by me.

"Never. I have hardly even been to the theatre. I saw some shows in Belfast, but they were lighthearted things. And before, in London, I only remember going once. My mother preferred to live very quietly. But we did take Robby to see *Peter Pan,* and he was enchanted. He still talks about it."

"From your smile, I would say you enjoyed it yourself."

His laughter drove away the last shadows of the strained look he has borne since his mother died. "I did, tremendously, though I must have been sixteen years old and would not have admitted it for the world."

The lift arrived, and Antoine pulled back the grille. I swung in on my crutches. Edmund followed. My heart thumped and my breath came unsteadily, as if I had ascended a mountain. We were going out together for the evening, for the first time.

Outside, the air was warm with the sweet scent of spring. The horses flicked their tails and tossed their heads as if they would like to carry us off into the country. I wish I had let them. I would give much to be alone with Edmund in a rural paradise tonight.

At the opera house, he helped me find a way through the crowd in the foyer to our seats. There were as many stairs as ever, but my old excitement at the prospect of witnessing the performance of a virtuoso had returned, and the difficulties were simply obstacles to be overcome. We were surrounded by the rustles and whispers of Parisian society, but from the moment the house lights went out, I was conscious of nothing but Edmund beside me and the passion on stage. Mme. Rossakova could have been singing only for us.

She was not, however—she was also singing for four hundred others, who massed around us in a screech of chatter in the interval. I glimpsed a familiar head, its hair carefully dressed to conceal a thin patch, and I caught Edmund's arm to keep him back.

"My friend Claude is here, the gentleman who first interviewed you. Do you remember?"

"Certainly." Edmund scanned the crowd.

"If we go the other way, we shall not have to greet him."

His face clouded. "You don't want him to see us together?"

"Oh, it isn't that! I only thought you might be shy."

In truth, I did not want to share Edmund's company. I did not want him smiling on Claude or on anyone but me. Such possessiveness is unappealing, I know, and I will not always feel so, but at that moment it seemed to me that our relation was a delicate shoot poking up through stony ground with only the smallest chance of finding the sun, and I must shelter it at any cost.

But he turned in Claude's direction. "No, I am not shy, and I see someone I know too—Chester Faukes from the American Red Cross. I must say good evening to him. Oh, but they are talking. How strange that they should know each other."

So Claude had made the most of his opportunity to reconnect with his American friend. I tightened my hold on Edmund's sleeve.

"Wait, I must explain. It is not a coincidence. They have known each other for some time. It was Mr. Faukes who first recommended you to Claude."

"How kind of him!" Edmund seemed even more eager to press through the crowd towards them.

"And it was also he who told us your name—I mean Ingreham."

That checked him for a moment. "He knows about Charles?"

"I don't think so. He had only seen your passport. But even if he does, it is better to admit something like that than to let it fester in your mind as a hidden shame. People will talk at first, perhaps, but they soon forget." I negotiated a corner step. "Claude does not know about your move to my apartment, but I must ask you again to call me James. I should like him to see us as equals, as friends."

Edmund's eyes danced. "Very well, James."

The sound of my name on his lips lit a fire deep inside me, as if it were a secret we shared.

At Edmund's gentle insistence, the crowd made way for my crutches, and we joined Claude and his American friend. I was unwilling to break the spell of this magical evening with idle talk, so I hung back. Claude did not speak of the opera, but of his latest cultural enthusiasm, a long and — so he said — revolutionary novel written by the rebellious daughter of a member of the Académie des Beaux-Arts.

"You must read her, both of you," he said. "All of France must read her — and then the rest of the world. We must have her translated into every language."

Chester Faukes seemed at ease with Claude and smiled indulgently at his wild gesticulations, which bodes well for their future. Chester brought Edmund up-to-date with events at the Red Cross office, while Claude said to me in a low voice, "You will forgive me if I do not ask you to supper tonight, *mon cher*?"

"Of course. I should prefer you do not."

"Ah, your relations are perhaps at the same tender stage?"

"Perhaps," I said, although I did not like the comparison. Surely Claude does not feel as I feel. Surely no one has ever felt as I feel! How could people go on complaining of the weather or the price of fish if they had once experienced this clarity, this certainty, this joy?

I moved closer to Edmund. They were now discussing the performance.

"I don't mind telling you I found it hard to follow," Chester said. "If I hadn't had the programme, I'd have been in the dark. I don't know a word of Italian. What about you?"

Edmund blushed. "I understand a little. I looked at it yesterday, and there are many similarities with Latin when you see it on the page."

"Ah yes, you were reading the libretto," I said to him. I had seen him with the book in his hand, but to tease him I added, "I saw that you did not put it back exactly where it belongs."

His colour deepened, and he narrowed his eyes at me in a warning. He need not have worried. I had no intention of telling them about the other book.

The bell rang, and we made our way back to our seats for the high drama of the last two acts. Despite the marvellous performance, I should not have minded if they had omitted the penultimate scene, in which Aïda does not appear. I was eager to be alone with Edmund, to have him look at me instead of the stage and know what he thought and felt and dreamed.

The final duet of the doomed lovers came at last. I glanced at Edmund's face and saw tears shining in his eyes. His gloved hand lay on his thigh. On an impulse I reached for it and covered it with my own.

He gave me a quick smile of gratitude. At the same time, he rolled his hand over and squeezed mine—only for a second, but joy rang out in my soul like the sweet song of a nightingale. Then the pressure was gone, and my hand returned to the armrest with no conscious effort on my part, as if his touch was too thrilling to be borne for more than a moment.

After that, nothing could get me home soon enough. I chafed at the crowd that hindered our passage to the door and was jealous of Claude, seated further back, who reached the exit with Chester a full two minutes before us.

The horses tossed their heads and snorted a welcome as we approached. "They know you," Edmund said. "Look how happy they are to see you."

"They are happy to know they can now trot home to their supper. I do not mistake that for affection."

Edmund laughed. "I am afraid you are a cynic."

How he has changed! He would not have dreamed of making such a personal remark a month or two ago. I bless whoever or whatever inspired me to make that settlement without requiring anything in return, for it has put us on an equal footing.

As the carriage carried us homeward, he gazed out at the light and laughter of the pavement cafés. To get his attention, I said, "A wonderful performance."

Had he heard? He did not look round. But after a moment he said, "Yes. I was enthralled." Then he turned to me, clasping his hands together. "Would you mind if we do not talk about it yet? I don't want to break the spell by racking my brains for something intelligent to say."

"Of course." If the performance had roused his emotions, I did not want to drive them away with intellectual conversation. I said nothing else but leaned back against the seat and closed my eye.

However, I was far from sleepy. My whole being was alert to every movement of Edmund's. With him beside me, I was a thousand times more alive. Every gesture he had made this evening, every nuance of his expression, had burrowed into my heart.

The apartment was dark and silent. Parkin was out, and Henri had long gone home. Antoine, who had worked the lift for us, offered to come in "to light the lamps and make you comfortable," but the lamps are electric and only require the flick of a switch, and we did not need a fire, so I refused. I did not want his interference. I wanted to be alone with Edmund.

"Supper should be laid for us," I said to Edmund, pulling off my hat and gloves as he closed the door.

It was—Parkin had left cold chicken, salad, bread, and wine—but we did not eat much. We sat side by side, and as I served him and smelled the food, I knew my stomach did not want it. I was too agitated, and yet I did not want the evening to end.

Edmund stopped me helping him to much meat. "Perhaps some bread," he said. We ate that and drank a little wine. We had not put many lights on, and the silent, dark apartment was an enchanted space.

"Well, I think I will say good night." Edmund rose. "Shall I clear these things away?"

"No, leave it for Parkin. He will return in an hour or two, I imagine."

"I do not mind doing it."

"*He* will mind. Let him do his work—he enjoys it."

He smiled to himself and said quietly, "As do I."

"You enjoy your work?"

"Yes."

"I am glad of it." The words came nowhere near describing the warmth I felt.

He covered the food but left it all on the table. I reached for my crutches and stood. At the doorway, he gave a long look back into the room. I wondered what he was thinking, but I did not know how to ask.

We went down the corridor towards the bedrooms, his steps matching my clunk and swing. I felt a sweet sadness. The evening was over — or was it? When he met my gaze, I thought perhaps it was not. His eyes held a light I had not seen before.

He opened the door of my room for me and put his hand inside to turn on the light. I leaned against the doorframe, propped my crutches against the wall, and caught his hand as it came back out.

"Will you stay a moment?" I pleaded.

He became very still. He blinked and looked down at the hand I held as if it did not belong to him. My fingertips caressed the back of it. He did not move or look away but watched as I stroked his fingers. He had taken off his gloves, and the contact of flesh on flesh sent blood careering through my veins.

Words welled up from some deep place in my heart or soul. "It is wonderful to have you living here, Edmund — although *wonderful* is not the right word because it implies something strange and unexpected. What I feel *is* strange and unexpected, but having you here seems the most natural thing in the world."

I hardly knew what I meant myself, but he seemed to understand. "Yes," he whispered, still gazing down at our hands.

Tiny hairs had risen on the side of his neck. I bent my head and kissed the place, then brushed it with my tongue.

He drew in a sharp breath and turned his head. His chin bumped my nose. "Oh! I am sorry —"

"Shh." I brought my mouth close to his and waited. As I hoped, he tipped his head and pressed his lips to mine.

He would have drawn away again at once, I think, but now I had him, I would not let go so easily. I cupped my hand around his neck, at the sensitive base of the skull where his hair is shortest, and drew him back into the kiss.

He came willingly. His warm breath smelled of cinnamon. His lips were cool and dry, and my whole existence converged on those slivers of tender skin meeting mine.

I moved my arm to bring him closer. My elbow hit my crutches, knocking them to the floor with a clatter. He pulled away from me and glanced down at them.

"Leave them." My voice came from my throat, hasty and hoarse.

Now his eyes met mine, glowing. His mouth was fixed in a smile, as if our first kiss had changed its shape forever.

He kept his body several inches clear of me, but he bent his head and brought his mouth to mine. Already he was more confident, more eager.

I put a hand on his lower back and drew him close until his firm member brushed against mine through our clothing, making my every nerve tingle.

He wanted me.

Then he jerked his hips away. I let him keep an inch of distance there, but he did not end the kiss. His lips kept returning to mine, like the lips of a drunkard who cannot let ten seconds go by without taking another sip of wine. I ran my tongue slowly around their inner surface. He quivered. Then the warm, wet tip of his tongue met mine, and a sunburst of flame lit my core.

After a minute or two, I increased the pressure of my hand on his back—not so much that it would force him to me, but enough to show him what I wanted. Little by little he came closer, until nothing separated us. His hardness pressed against my thigh. I shifted to have it at the most pleasurable place, and the flames in me flared higher.

His lips trembled on mine, and I dared to move a little more. He did not pull away. Then his need took over. With one hand he gripped my uninjured shoulder, his other hand went to my hip, and he rubbed against me, hard.

Blood rushed through my veins as he took control, but within seconds it was over. His breath caught and stopped, his back stiffened, and a tremor went through him. Then he wrenched himself from my arms and rushed away towards his room.

I was left teetering on my one leg. If I hadn't immediately pressed my hands flat on the wall, I would have fallen. I called sharply, "Edmund! My crutches!"

"One moment—I will be back!"

I tried to control my racing heart and the angry throb of my unsatisfied desire. I was not altogether successful, and my frustration must have been evident when he returned from his bedroom. It only began to die away when I saw the thick, flat protrusion in the front of his trousers. He had padded them.

He must have reached ecstasy in that brief contact—my kiss had excited him so much—and he had run for handkerchiefs to absorb the wetness from his undergarments and protect his new suit.

Why did I find this so touching? It melted all my frustration in an instant.

His face was pink when he picked up my crutches and handed them to me. He did not meet my gaze. I thanked him and took a step into my room.

He spoke from the threshold, as if unwilling to cross it. "Do you need anything else?"

I knew I must not detain him then. I must let him retreat into his burrow. "No, thank you. I can manage very well, now that my shoulder is better."

"Then good night, James."

"Good night, Edmund. Sleep well."

One flashing smile, and he was gone.

An experienced man would have come to my bed. He would not have taken his own pleasure and left me. But I did not mind. I treasure his lack of experience. I will treat it tenderly.

I could not sleep, so after a time I turned on the lamp and brought out this book to record my happiness. I have never felt a contentment so profound. All the world, all my thoughts, sparkle with starlight.

Edmund feels something for me—not as I once was, or as I will be, but now, as I am, with my pinned-up trouser leg, my crutches, and my eye patch. Edmund wants me! He truly does. He could not have been acting. He was clumsy and uncertain. I felt him tremble in my arms.

My Edmund.

40

James's Journal
Sunday, May 4th

Edmund was all smiles and blushes at breakfast, and so, I believe, was I. I said nothing, however. I did not want to press him to greater and greater intimacies. I wanted to court him, to make him always want more, and for him to lead as often as me. I wanted to savour each step, each stage of his awakening. I thought I would have the time.

He had been to the early church service, and I had waited to have breakfast with him when he returned. Then I wanted to keep him near me, so I suggested we work on the book, even though it was Sunday, because we were so near the end.

He fetched his notebook with a light step and sunshine in his eyes, and we reached the final paragraph before Parkin announced luncheon.

I said with a flourish, "There! I believe it is finished."

Edmund gave me his warmest smile. "Congratulations, James."

"I could not have done it without you. This evening we must celebrate. I shall ask Henri to do his utmost for our dinner."

After lunch I went to the kitchen and ordered bisque, duck, and a light lemon mousse. I asked Parkin to fill the dining room with flowers and candles. Our dinner would celebrate not only the end of the book, but the start of our romance—our love. I dared to call it that, in my mind.

Edmund typed the last few pages in the afternoon. Then I dictated a letter to go to Claude with one copy of the text. Edmund had made a carbon copy of every page of every draft, and the library was now full of piles of paper. We took tea together there, after which I left Edmund to make a package of the book.

And then disaster fell.

I was practising on the piano in the salon, thinking I would ask him to sing for me before dinner, when there was a commotion in the hall outside. I stopped playing. A voice cried in French, "No, no, old man. I want to see him, and you will not stop me!"

My limbs went cold. The next moment, Loulou rushed into the room.

"James, *chéri*, I have been to see my villa. It is so pretty! I had to come and thank you."

His eyes were dark pools, his voice was high and quick, and his gestures were extravagant. He had taken his drug. I glanced at the library doors. They were closed, but Louis spoke loudly.

I closed the piano and stood up, supporting myself on the lid. "Be quiet, Louis. You should not be here."

"But why? I only want to show you how much I appreciate your gift."

He came right up to me and put a hand on my shoulder. I tried to push him away, but I could not do it without falling. Nor could I retreat, with the piano stool behind me.

Without thinking, I reached for the nearest bell. The sound rang out, but it should not have—Parkin's bell rings in the pantry. I had caught up Edmund's cowbell.

The library doors opened at once. Edmund took one step into the room and stopped. Louis was so close to me, we might have been in an embrace.

In desperation, I began, "This is not—"

Louis drowned me out. "But what is this? The secretary? You told me he had left France!"

"I did not mean forever!" I turned back to Edmund, who stood like a pillar of ice in the doorway, his face sheet-white. "Edmund, this is not what you think."

He did not look at me, but stared at Louis.

Louis stared back and took a step away from me. "I came only to thank the love of my life for his charming present, and what do I find? The secretary is here, dressed so elegantly! He is something more than a secretary now, is he not? And me, I must take the second place. I see it all. You banish me to the seaside, so you can visit me there when it suits you, while he enjoys life with you in Paris!"

"That is not it, Louis!" I roared. "I am finished with you. You signed a paper. You should not be here!"

Quick footsteps in the hall, and Parkin appeared with Antoine, who had rolled up his sleeves, prepared for battle.

Louis gave a high cackling laugh. "Ha! Now *monsieur le concierge* arrives—your lion, come to defend you—but he sleeps too much, you know! One can easily find a way in without waking him!"

Antoine growled. He gripped Loulou's wrist and pulled him away from me. Parkin stood behind them, holding a thick cane.

"Do not come here again, Louis," I warned, as Antoine dragged him to the door.

"I will not! Do not fear it! If you prefer that thin, bloodless specimen of an Englishman to me, Louis Duquesne, you are not worth another thought. I spit on your villa!"

He matched action to word, and spat on the floor.

I turned to Edmund, but the doorway was empty.

I went looking for him at once. He was not in the library, so I swung myself down the corridor with a heavy heart.

His door was closed. I knocked. No reply.

"Edmund? I am sorry you had to witness that. He had undertaken not to come. I ended things with him months ago, as I told you." Silence. "Please open the door, and I will explain. It is over, damn it."

He did not answer.

"May I come in?"

Nothing stirred. Was he there? I turned the handle. Yes, the door was locked, so he must be inside. Perhaps he had been badly upset and did not want me to see it.

"Edmund, I am so sorry. Please come out soon, and we will talk."

I stood there a little longer, but there was no sound from within. Defeated, I went slowly back to the salon and resumed my practice at the piano. My light touch was gone. I began playing something melancholy, but frustration and anger rose inside me until it became a cacophony of crashing keys.

Life is so unjust! I did all I could to treat Louis well, and still he has trampled on the beautiful, sensitive bud of affection that was growing between me and Edmund.

It will rise again. I have to believe that. It is not dead.

It is far from dead in me, in any case.

When Parkin appeared in the salon an hour or two later, I was sitting with a book, reading the same page over and over without taking anything in.

I said, "You must have a glass panel put in the door, so you can see who is there before you open it."

"Yes, sir. I am terribly sorry. He pushed past me, and—"

I cut him off. "I know. I heard him."

He cleared his throat. "Dinner is served."

"Have you called Edmund—Mr. Ingreham?"

"Yes, sir. He is not hungry."

"Then dinner can go to hell." I turned my head away, but Parkin did not leave. "What is it?"

"Pardon me for saying so, but if it does, Henri will go with it."

"What? Oh, you mean Henri will give notice if I do not eat?"

I threw the book down on the couch. It is all very well having servants, but they come with responsibilities. Two or three servants can be harder to manage than a whole battalion of soldiers. With soldiers, one only has to think of their physical welfare. With servants, one must also consider their feelings.

"All right, but take away the damned flowers before I go in."

"I have done so, sir."

I sat in the chilly dining room alone. Henri's signature dishes came out one by one, beautifully presented. Edmund should have been with me, his eyes sparkling, his shy smile lighting up his face, relishing the food and my company. Instead, all I had to cheer me was a bottle of wine, and it did a poor job. I grew gloomier with each glass.

I ate three spoonfuls of soup and a slice of duck. I could not face the lemon mousse. Everything tasted like ashes.

I crumpled my napkin on the table and told Parkin to do what he could with the remains, without letting Henri know. "Take a plate to Mr. Ingreham, have some for your supper, give it to the poor . . . whatever you can think of."

"Yes, sir."

I sat up for several hours after dinner, imagining a family of ragged children enjoying roast duck and lobster bisque like Dickens's Cratchits, and I the lonely Scrooge. The evening passed without sight or sound of Edmund. When I came to bed, the plate still sat outside his door. I lifted the cover. He had not touched the food.

I cannot sleep. My emotions are a bewildering mess of grief and resentment. He is so stubborn. Why will he not let me explain?

I shall take half a powder. Parkin has left me one or two in the box, though I no longer need them for pain.

41

Edmund's Journal
Sunday, May 4th

I have been such a fool. He is still seeing Louis Duquesne.

He called through my bedroom door that it was over, and perhaps it is, now, but they must have been together while I was in Switzerland. Duquesne knew I had been out of France. Now James turns him away because he has bought me instead.

"You signed a paper," James bellowed at him. I also signed a paper. *In full and final settlement.*

My heart is torn to shreds.

Why do I feel this way? It makes no sense. Six weeks ago, I offered James exactly this—myself, to replace Duquesne—and I longed for him to accept. I will admit that now. It was not a sacrifice, not something I did in desperation, for Robby's sake. I *wanted* to be his kept man.

But so much has changed since then. I believed he cared. I thought the light in his eye and the smile on his lips meant this was more than a passing attraction. He settled money on me—so generously, it seemed. Now my conscience tells me I must give it back, and what will become of Robby?

How I wish I had never accepted it!

James said he gave me those funds to make me independent. He said he did not intend to trap me, and I believed him. I went beyond desiring him and began to love him. I thought it was safe to let him into my heart. Last night — was it only last night? — I even hoped he might feel the same. I had a glimpse of heaven, only to come crashing to the ground.

Tears fill my eyes. All those dreams, built on one kiss. How could I have been so blind?

Oh, but what a kiss it was! I shall never have another like it . . .

42

James's Journal
Monday, May 5th

I awoke this morning in an optimistic mood. My heart had forgotten yesterday and remembered only the evening before, when we went to the theatre and kissed, though my head knew full well what had happened since.

All that mattered was that I loved Edmund . . . and he must love me in return, I thought, or something close to it, or yesterday would not have hurt him so badly. I would see him at breakfast and put everything right. I would hold his hand, look into his eyes, and explain about Louis. He would understand.

Then I sat up and found my morning tea cold beside my bed, its surface covered with a slithering skin. The powder had made me sleep late.

I rang for Parkin, who brought fresh tea and told me it was past ten o'clock. My spirits sank. Edmund would have breakfasted long ago.

"What is Mr. Ingreham doing?"

"I believe he has gone out, sir."

I nodded. He often goes for walks. I told myself it meant nothing. I drank my tea in bed while Parkin fetched hot water and prepared my shaving things.

I do not usually face my reflection in the glass until I am shaved, brushed, equipped with my eye patch, and ready for the day, but today I looked at once. I was not a pleasant sight. My skin was mottled, my chin rough, my hair wild. The empty eye socket was like a grim, sunken cave, pulling my brow out of shape. The remaining eye was bloodshot.

All my optimism drained away. This was what Edmund would see every morning if we spent our nights together. How could I have imagined he might care for me? No doubt he had closed his eyes when he kissed me, and his passion had been nothing but a physical response. Men of his age are easily aroused.

I spent a dull morning. Parkin brought me hot chocolate, but it did not cheer me. Outside it was raining, a grey drizzle that made passersby hurry along the street below my windows, huddled into their coats. Why would he walk so long in such weather?

At lunchtime I asked Parkin, "Has Mr. Ingreham returned?"

"No, sir." His voice was low and gentle. He blames Louis for upsetting Edmund, I think, and not me. Perhaps he even blames himself a little for letting Louis push his way in.

I took my place at the table. "He moves so quietly. Might he not have come back without our hearing?"

"He does not have a key."

"All the same . . . did you look in his room?"

"Yes, sir."

"You opened the door? You did not simply knock?"

"I looked inside a few minutes ago, and also in the library."

"His door was not locked?"

"No."

Parkin presented me with a dish of two grilled fish. Their eyes gazed out balefully from their bed of herbs, as if they had known and accepted their fate.

I pushed at the platter. "I do not want that. Take it away and bring me bread and cheese."

He covered the fish and brought the cheese board. "Wine, sir?"

"No, only water." I watched his veined hand fill my water glass. "What did he say to you when he went out?"

"I didn't see him go, sir."

"Then did he say anything at breakfast? Anything at all?"

"Mr. Ingreham said very little this morning, but I formed the impression that he intended to go to the cemetery."

"To visit his mother's grave?" I took a slice of bread and cut myself some cheese. "Surely he would not have stayed so long."

"It's possible he's gone to see a friend from his old district."

"I did not know he had friends there," I said with bitterness. "He tells you more than he tells me."

"He didn't tell me so, sir. I inferred it from the fact that he was wearing his old suit at breakfast."

I put down my knife. Why would he wear his old suit? Dread clutched at my heart. "Was he carrying a bag when he left?"

"I don't know, sir. As I believe I mentioned, I didn't see him go."

I took up my crutches and made my way to Edmund's room without another word. His mother's photograph was gone from beside the bed, and there was nothing else of his to be seen.

My breath caught, and I put a shaky hand to my heart. I went to the wardrobe and flung open the door.

It was all right. His clothes were still there.

I was weak with relief. He keeps his room so tidy that it looks bleak and empty without him, but he will be back.

He must have slipped the photograph into his pocket for comfort and put on his old suit to... to avoid appearing wealthy, I suppose. To discourage pickpockets, perhaps, or because he did not want to parade his new status in front of old acquaintances.

I locked the door and hid the key in my own room, so he cannot come and go without my knowledge.

In the afternoon, they came to fit the finished false leg. I had been waiting for this with such anticipation, and yet I would have forgotten if Parkin had not reminded me. Tomorrow I shall have my glass eye, but first it was the leg.

The doctor introduced the craftsman who has made this masterpiece of mechanics. It has an odd appearance, for in places it has been thickened out with plaster to mirror the shape of my other leg, while at the ankle and toe joints only the metal skeleton shows. But covered by a sock, it looks real. And it fits. It matches the other for height, and it works.

I can stand. I can get up off the couch without a crutch, as long as I sit near the arm rest. I can walk!

I cannot describe the feeling of being on two feet for the first time in nine months, even if one of the feet is not my own. I was mad with exhilaration, as if I had taken some of Louis's drug.

I am free! I can go where I wish, without depending on servants and friends. I am not trapped on couches and in wheeled chairs. Outside I will need a cane, and I must pay special attention on stairs and cobbles and after rain, when the paths may be slippery. But in the apartment, if I am careful, I shall need no support at all.

I stumbled awkwardly around the salon at first, fearful of losing my balance. In the moment when I lift my own foot to step forward, all my weight rests on this hinged appendage that cannot feel the floor. The doctor told me I must trust it and move as naturally as possible to avoid stressing the other joints. I went more slowly, and then it was easier. I must practise, he says, and not expect to stride out like an uninjured man. I must have patience — never my strongest virtue!

They expressed satisfaction with the fit, congratulating me before they left, although it was all their own work. I walked to my room — unsteadily, but without crutches! — where Parkin helped me dress in the trousers that have hung in the wardrobe waiting for this moment.

"I really think nobody would guess," I said when I had taken a few steps back and forth before the looking glass. "I will always have a limp, but many men limp on their own two feet."

"Yes, sir." His voice faltered. I gave him a sharp glance, and he added, "Excuse me, sir, but I am so glad!"

He had tears in his eyes, the dear old thing.

I stayed at the glass for a time after he had gone. Except for the eye patch, I look much as I did before the war. I am older, of course, and pain has etched more lines on my face than my thirty years deserve, but I have kept my shape through these long months of inactivity. It did not seem too much to hope that a man might feel something for me.

I showed the leg to Henri when he came in from his afternoon break. He has only a solid wooden peg, and he was most admiring of the foot and the way it moves at the ankle.

"We shall have you fitted for one just like it," I said. "What do you think of that?"

He looked doubtful. "I don't know, sir. I've had my piece of wood for a few years now, and I'm accustomed to it."

I let him go, but I have not given up the idea. I shall convince him. Parkin will be making an appointment for him in a week or two.

Now Parkin has brought tea, and I am resting while I write. I cannot walk for long stretches because of the pressure on the fleshy end of my leg, which is not used to carrying my weight. But that will pass.

I only wish Edmund were here to see it. What a surprise he will have when he comes in! He will forget his anger and be happy for me, and then he cannot refuse to listen to my explanation. He will forgive me, I know he will, and my joy will be complete.

Later

I waited and waited. He did not come. All my pleasure in walking drained away drop by drop through the evening, to be replaced by a gnawing worry.

A sound at the salon door—I turned, but it was only Parkin.

"He is not here?" I asked.

"No, sir."

"It must be past eleven."

"It is almost midnight, sir."

"Then you should be in bed. You know I do not need you at night." My voice was sharper than he deserved, but I could not bear to see him looking so sorry for me.

"I thought you might want help with the leg, this first time."

"Oh . . . the leg. Yes, I suppose I do."

I got to my feet and winced at the pain.

"Shall I take it off here, sir, and bring your crutches?"

"No." I took a step. Daggers shot through my flesh. I sat back down. "Well, yes, perhaps that would be better."

"That's right. You've left it on too long, no doubt."

They had told me only two or three hours, the first day. "I wanted him to see it," I said like a fractious child.

"I know, sir, and he will tomorrow, I expect."

"You don't think he will be back tonight?"

"Not now, I don't suppose."

Where was Edmund? What was he doing? Would he ever come back? Was he punishing me? Or had something terrible happened?

Parkin stood at my side, patient as ever. I pulled up my trouser leg, and he unfastened the straps of the prosthesis. He lifted my own shortened leg to look at the end of it in the light, tutting over it.

"Have I broken the skin?"

"No, sir, but it's all red, and there's some swelling. I'll fetch your ointment."

He came back with that and my pyjamas.

"Where is he, Parkin?"

"I don't know, sir."

I thought of Edmund wandering the streets and being hit by a tram or falling under a carriage. I thought of men in alleys with knives. An icy finger of dread ran down my spine.

"Did you ever discover his address in Auteuil?" I asked as Parkin rubbed ointment into my stump.

"No. I didn't think you wanted me to go on with that."

"You were right, I did not at the time, but now I wish you had. He might have met with an accident, and we would not know."

Parkin helped my into my pyjamas. "No, sir, this is his registered address now. The authorities would send word here."

"You are sure of that?"

"Yes, he changed it as soon as he came back from Switzerland. The people where he was before would have reported him gone, you see."

That was some comfort. French bureaucracy can be infuriating, but they do insist on everything being up-to-date. So his papers would show this apartment as his address, and Edmund is not the kind of man who might forget to carry his papers. If he were lying dead or unconscious somewhere, we would have heard.

Unless his papers were stolen . . .

Parkin adjusted my pyjama leg to prevent it rubbing on the sore place. "Don't worry, sir. He'll have stayed with his friends, I expect."

"What friends? He has never said anything about them to me. Do you know who they are?"

"Not to speak of. He mentioned his landlady once or twice, but I don't believe he ever told me her name."

There is Chester Faukes, of course, but I do not think Edmund and Chester are close. When we met at the opera, they gave no sign of knowing each other well. Besides, if he wanted to hide from me, he would surely not go to a friend of Claude's.

Parkin followed me to my room, carrying my clothes and the false leg. I sat on the bed and watched him putting everything to rights.

"I do not know what I should do without you, Parkin."

"You'd manage, sir." But he smiled to himself, as if he knew I wouldn't manage half so well. "Let me get you a powder to help you sleep."

"I don't want it. I had one last night." And it had let Edmund get away.

"Very good, sir, but don't go tossing and turning all night. That leg needs a rest, or you'll be back on crutches for another few months. I'll leave the powder here, in case you want it later. Shall I put out the light?"

"No, I will sit up and write for a time."

He went to the door. "Good night, then, sir."

"Good night, Parkin. Oh, I have the key to his room."

Parkin raised one eyebrow a fraction, but I took no notice of that.

"You'll have to wake me if he returns."

"Yes, sir." He left me, and I took out this book.

Where is Edmund now? Has he stayed the night with a friend I do not know, or gone to an hotel, or picked up a stranger in the Bois to punish me?

I never imagined love would bring me so much pain, or be so fraught with worry.

Night

I lay awake for a long time after writing those last words. Then I got up and reached for my crutches.

Taking the key to Edmund's room, I made my way down the corridor. He could not be there ... or could he? What if he had a secret set of keys? I had to be sure.

I unlocked the door and opened it a crack. A faint light showed inside. My heart leaped.

But no. It was only the moon, shining through the unshuttered window. His room was empty, his bed smoothly made, exactly as it had been in the morning.

I opened the wardrobe. His clothes were my reassurance, promising that he would be back. I ran my fingers over the fabrics in the moonlight, feeling them soft against my skin. This was the suit he wore to the opera. This he was wearing when I took him in my arms.

I do not know how long I stood there, resting my cheek against his empty clothes. At last I closed the wardrobe, pushing it to with one finger. The latch clicked closed, and at the same time, something clicked in my mind.

I froze. Then I snatched at the handle and pulled the door open again. I flicked through the hangers in a frenzy. I lifted a crutch and swiped at the far wall until I succeeded in turning on the electric light. I stared into the wardrobe. Then I went to the chest of drawers. Underclothes lay there, yes, but all new, all Parisian. Nothing old or worn, nothing homemade, nothing with an English or Irish label.

Could he have thrown them out? Discarded the old when he had the new? But no, it was not like him to do that. He was careful, thrifty. He'd have gone on wearing the old things until they fell apart, keeping the new ones for best.

I moved to the washstand and opened the drawer. Empty. No shaving things. And no letters, no papers, none of the clutter of life anywhere in the room.

He had gone, taking what he came with and rejecting all that he had bought with the money I gave him.

He had left me.

The shock hit me like an icy waterfall. I sat down on his bed, shivering.

Since he first crossed my threshold in January, life had slowly taken on some meaning. I had found a purpose. I had imagined a future. I had even, for a few hours, felt joy. All gone.

Gone, and I had never told him how much I cared for him.

I sat there until the moonlight was replaced by the first grey fingers of dawn. Then I had a thought that comforted me—the money. He would not want to keep it all. He would have to discuss it with me, and then I could tell him how I felt.

I clutched at this idea, repeating it over to myself. *He will come about the money. I will see him again soon.* That raised my spirits a little, and I came back to my own room.

I must try to sleep. I shall tell myself that when I wake, Edmund will be here. He must be.

43

Edmund's Journal
Tuesday, May 6th, early hours

I fled the apartment after breakfast, wearing my old suit. I packed my things and brought them with me, so I will never have to go back.

I did not bring the new clothes. They are his, not mine. I could not bear to wear them again, or even to see them hanging in another room. I have turned my back on everything he bought me — except the programme from the opera. I did keep that. But I pushed it to the bottom of my bag, and there it stays. I cannot look at it.

First I took fresh flowers to the cemetery. The air was damp with a thin warm rain that slowly soaked me through, but it was not unpleasant. The trees were full of chirruping birds. All nature is in blossom, and I am in turmoil.

At her grave I talked to Mama as I never did in life. I told her how women have never moved me and men always have. I poured out all my longing for James, and how my heart had been cut open when I understood that he, with all his experience, cannot be expected to feel the same.

Perhaps he did end his arrangement with Louis Duquesne some months ago. Parkin told me at breakfast that Duquesne was never in the apartment while I was in Switzerland. They must have met elsewhere, and Parkin thinks it was by chance.

But it makes no difference when the affair ended. It was over, so James needed another outlet. It could have been anyone. He turned to me because I was there and willing—more than willing, to my shame.

I locked myself in my room at his apartment all last night. He might have thought I was angry or jealous, and I was, for the first hour. Then the rage left me, and I was only afraid—afraid to see him, afraid even to speak to him through the door, because I knew I should be lost if I did.

I miss him so much already—his smile, his courage, his acceptance of himself as he is. I might have learned some of that from him. But if I go back, we will act on our desires, and I will fall deeper and deeper in love. And a time will come—perhaps very soon—when he will cast me off with my *full and final settlement* and break my heart. Is it worth it?

My body shouts *Yes, yes, yes!*—my mind says *No*. When I am with him, I would give all my future happiness for one kiss, but when I am away from him, I fear I would regret that kiss for the rest of my life.

From the cemetery, I went to our church. The organist was playing, but otherwise the church was deserted—empty of people, filled with music. I slipped into a pew and prayed for help to see my right path.

Did God send Louis Duquesne as a warning to save me, to show me that what I wanted was wrong and could not end happily? Or have I reacted too strongly? Am I being unfair to James?

I know what the chaplain would say if I confided in him, which I shall not do—that James is a temptation I must avoid. But the chaplain is not God. God is love and can see our hearts.

Would He have made me this way, if He did not mean me to love as I do?

But we could use that argument to justify anything. A violent man might say, "Would God have given me this temper, if He did not mean me to beat my wife?"

No, it is different—God wants us to love each other, not to cause each other pain.

But love is one thing, and the carnal expression of it is another.

Oh, I do not know. I have lost all sense of right and wrong.

I do not believe it would be a sin if James felt as deeply as I do, but I cannot convince myself that he does.

I prayed for a sign, but nothing came—except that once, when the music swelled and rose to the heavens, I seemed to hear a voice deep in my mind. It held no emotion, as if it was simply pointing out a fact, but it overwhelmed every other sound. The organ faded to a distant accompaniment. I was filled with a profound sense of peace, and knew that all would be well if I trusted this voice.

The voice told me, *You are in the wrong place.*

Was it the voice of God, or the voice of my own heart? And what did it mean? That the church was the wrong place, and James's apartment would be right? Or that Paris is the wrong place, and I must go far away?

I compromised and came to our old house.

Mme. H. was in a convivial mood, wanting to hear all about Robby and tell me the latest news of the district. Her little granddaughter has come back to live with her — a sweet, toddling thing who consoles her somewhat for the loss of her daughter.

Mama's old room was free, so I have taken it for the night. I hoped to find some comfort where she spent so many hours. I thought a vestige of her spirit might still be here to encourage me, but no. I do not feel her quiet presence as I sometimes do at the cemetery. I only feel the lack of it. Without her pretty things, this room is just like the others — threadbare rug, chipped ewer, and scuffed dark furniture. Mama with all her delicacy might never have been here.

I ate dinner with the tenants. Only the Russians were familiar. The rest are new. But all the circumstances — the room, the food, the sound of cutlery scraping on the plates, Mme. H.'s remarks as she served us — all these were exactly as they used to be. It was hard to bear. I felt I had woken from a dream of light and colour to find myself back in the dreary, lonely toil of real life.

How wealth corrupts — and how quickly! It is so much harder to be poor, now I have had a taste of riches. So much harder to be alone, now I have had a taste of love . . .

But that is gone. A dream. I will think no more of it.

And Robby? What shall I do about him?

Perhaps I do not need to decide yet. His fees are paid for the time being. I might appeal to Lord Akingbourne once more, or to Mama's sister. One of them may be moved to help Robby now Mama is gone. If not, I must hope one summer in that pure air will cure him, for I cannot afford to keep him there longer.

I shall try to sleep, trusting that my way will become clear. I may hear the voice again, or receive some other sign, or see for myself what is the right thing to do.

44

James's Journal
Tuesday, May 6th

I woke the moment Parkin opened the door. I sat straight up in bed, but he had only brought my tea as usual.

"Not yet, sir," he said in answer to my unspoken question. "The eye doctor—"

"Will be here this morning. I know. Unless he has telephoned to change the appointment?"

"No, sir. He's coming at ten."

I breakfasted on toast and coffee and drew out the meal as long as I could. I watched by the window as ten o'clock approached—the time Edmund used to start work each Tuesday, Thursday, and Saturday—but only the oculist came.

The eye was fitted in no time, and De Smet showed me how to put it in and take it out. It is a terrible thing to have sitting in one's hand, big and white and staring, but when it is in, it fills the socket perfectly. He said I should only wear it indoors at first, until the muscles are accustomed to holding it in. If it fell out in the street it might break—not to mention the embarrassment of being suddenly eyeless in public.

I went to the glass and was astonished at what I saw. The false eye is controlled by the muscles within the socket, so it moves with the other eye, more or less. I thought the skin around the socket had been pulled permanently out of shape, but no. It takes up its old symmetry when the glass eye is in place. The shrapnel went clean into the eye without touching the lid, and unless one watches closely, my face appears uninjured.

Though I say it myself, I am more handsome than I thought possible.

All the same, the sight did not cheer me. What is the good of being handsome, if Edmund is not here to see me?

What good is anything, without him by my side?

My body has been through torture, and I bear the scars. Am I now to suffer a bitter torment of the heart and soul?

No. I shall call for my carriage and go to Auteuil.

45

James's Journal
Wednesday, May 7th

After writing those last words yesterday morning, I closed this book, took out the false eye, and set out to look for Edmund.

Parkin wanted to accompany me, but I would not let him. I did not dare wear my new leg, not knowing how many hours my search might take, but I had the coachman to assist me in and out of the carriage, and I wanted no more help than that.

Seeing the district reminded me of the time I had taken Edmund and Robert home from the Bois. The carriage stopped in the same square. There was the street name, the Rue Michel-Ange, and my heart gave a jump at the sight of it, even though I now knew that Edmund had never lived at number thirty-eight.

I went there first, however, and asked the stationer if "Monsieur Vaughan" had been in.

The man's eyes flicked over my clothes as if assessing my status before he nodded. "He collected his mail this morning."

"Ah!" If only I had come earlier . . . but I was on his trail! "Were there many letters for him?"

The stationer drew away. Perhaps my desperate hunger for information showed, though I had spoken as casually as I could. I took a banknote from my pocket and tapped it on the counter.

He gave it a sidelong glance and admitted, "Only one."

"Did you notice the return address?"

"No, monsieur." He gave a regretful shrug. "But it was not a foreign letter. It had a French stamp, and it had arrived by the first post this morning."

I asked if he knew where the Vaughans had lived, but he only repeated what he'd told Parkin—that he thought they were nearby. Did he know in which direction? He did not, so I let him have the banknote and left.

I began my campaign full of energy and determination, certain that Edmund was not far off—perhaps even within hearing if I had dared to shout, but I did not want to embarrass him. I advanced along the Rue Michel-Ange, asking who let rooms and braving the iron grilles to attack one guardian after another.

But male or female, owner or concierge, old or relatively young, they all gave the same shrug and denied knowing an English family named Ingreham or Vaughan. After a time, I had a ludicrous sense of déjà vu, as if I were meeting the same person over and over again. My shoulder ached, and I could not face another embodiment of the spirit of France without sustenance.

I considered going home for lunch in case Edmund had returned, but it was not likely, and I preferred not to see Parkin until my objective was achieved. So I returned to the square. Two cafés faced each other on opposite corners, both with a line of chairs and tables under the awning on the pavement. One had a solitary drinker, the other was half full. Which?

I wanted to do what Edmund would do. Perhaps he would come to take his lunch, and I could talk to him on neutral ground. Would he choose the better-frequented place like a Frenchman, or would he take pity on the failing café, even if its emptiness showed that the food was bad? The latter, I thought, and went to the empty one.

They had not heard of him—perhaps he did not go to cafés—but I chose a table inside, by the window, where I could see but not be seen. I ordered onion soup with cheese to follow, thinking the worst cook could not go wrong with that. It came almost at once, and I ate quickly.

Refreshed, I went outside. I had covered the Rue Michel-Ange. I could try the roads to the east or the west. There seemed nothing to choose between the two, but as I surveyed the terrain, the woman I had questioned in the café came out and pointed eastwards. "Try down there. Full of boardinghouses, and all very respectable."

I thanked her and went in that direction. Again I met with a *"Non"* at every door, but I sensed that this was the right place, and as I moved along the row of houses, my heart began to beat a little faster.

Haussmann designed the arteries of that district, and his buildings are much the same anywhere in Paris. But the side roads were more ramshackle, with some of the old village houses still standing in the shadow of the new apartment blocks. This particular street had something indefinably Edmund about it—an air of respectable poverty, of struggling to swim rather than sink. I could picture him here.

At one house where I asked my questions, a stout woman in a cotton apron gave me the familiar "*Non.*" But as I turned away, she added, "You could ask at Madame Huguet's. She had some English in the winter."

She directed me up the road. I hurried as fast as my crutches would carry me and pulled at the doorbell. The door opened at once, as if somebody had been standing behind it.

"Madame Hu—"

The name died in my throat. Edmund stood before me. He wore a coat and hat, and his bag was in his hand.

He took a step back. A flush came to his cheeks. "Mr. Clarynton."

My heart thudded. I thought his eyes had lit up for a second, but now they were dull. I wanted to shout for joy at the sight of him, but his expression was far from welcoming, and he had not called me James.

"Where are you going?" I asked.

"To—" He swallowed. "I prefer not to say."

"Not to Switzerland, I hope?"

I meant it as a joke. I had thought only that the house must be full and he was moving to another. But the colour that flooded his face told me I had hit the mark.

My head spun, and I staggered. Had I found him only to lose him again?

"Don't go," I pleaded. "Not yet. Let us talk a little. I cannot let you leave with this misunderstanding between us."

He stared at me for a moment, and then he opened the door wider and I stepped in. He showed me into a grim, dark dining room, barely big enough to contain its long table and heavy sideboard, and smelling of cabbage. He motioned to me to sit down, but I preferred to stand.

"Let me explain about Louis. We met in the street—"

He waved my words away. "This has nothing to do with him, except that he made me see how the money would bind me. The settlement did not make me your equal but your dependant. I was wrong ever to think I could live as Louis Duquesne does—I would be too easily crushed. I need to keep my independence."

"But I was not asking you to give that up. I would not crush you!"

"I know you did not mean to, but that would have been the effect." His brow creased, but his voice softened. "I am sure you did everything with the best intentions, and it was very generous of you, but it is not what I want."

"And you would have left without speaking to me?" This hurt. Did I really mean so little to him?

He flushed. "I did not dare to see you, in case... You can be very persuasive. I would have written. I have written to Mr. Finlayson already, asking him to draw up whatever papers I must sign to return your gift to you."

Finlayson! Of course, Edmund could arrange things that way, and cut me out completely. It had not crossed my mind because I had not imagined he would go to such lengths to avoid me.

"You want to return all of it? But what about Robert?"

"I will seek other help for him."

"And if you do not find it?"

A flicker of pain crossed his face. "Then he will be in God's hands."

"Pshaw! Don't give me that nonsense when I have seen what God lets men do to each other with no aid or interference from Him. If God is up there at all, He has turned His back on us."

I should not have called his faith *nonsense*. His eyebrows set in a familiar stubborn line. "I do not agree, but I see no point in discussing it."

"And you," I went on, "how will you live?"

He chewed at his lip as if he knew I would not like what I was about to hear. "The Académie des Beaux-Arts has offered me a fee for the French-to-English translation of a substantial work."

"The Académie — Do you mean Claude? The traitor!" I cried. "Stealing you away!"

"James, please." He caught my arm. I had been brandishing a crutch and had almost smashed one of the ugly gas lamps fixed to the uglier papered wall. His grasp was strong, and his voice was firm. "There is no question of stealing. I do not belong to you."

"You have made that very clear," I muttered. "What does Claude want you to translate? Not the thing he was praising to the skies when we saw him at the opera?"

"Yes. He had read your book as soon as it arrived, and he was kind enough to say that he had been struck by the flow of the language. He evidently knows English quite well. And he had shown it to Chester, who said the same. Of course I told him you were the author and I could not claim any credit for it. But he asked me if I had not had some part in it. He read me a few examples, saying they did not sound like your voice, and I admitted I might have made one or two suggestions as to the phrasing."

"One or two suggestions! You damn near rewrote the thing."

Edmund shrugged that off. "At any rate, he knew the book was finished, so he thought you would not need me much longer and I might be glad of other work. There is no more to it than that."

"And when did you see Claude behind my back? Oh, the letter you collected this morning . . . Was that from him? He wrote to you here in Auteuil? Not at my apartment?"

"He did not know I was staying with you," Edmund reminded me. "Chester had given him the address in the Rue Michel-Ange. He wrote, and I went to see him at once."

It sounded as if Claude was seeing a good deal of Chester. No doubt his motives towards Edmund were honourable. All the same . . . "He might have telephoned to ask my"—*not permission*—"opinion."

"He said you had already told him so much about me that he did not need to ask you for a formal reference."

"Well." I wiped my overheated brow. If Edmund would be working for Claude, at least I would see him from time to time. "So you are visiting Robert before you start? When do you return? Will Claude find you an office?"

Edmund swallowed and did not meet my gaze. "I intend to do the work there."

"At the Académie des Beaux-Arts?"

"No, in Davos."

There was a pounding in my ears. "In *Switzerland*?" My tongue stumbled on the word as if swollen.

"Yes. I will find lodgings as my mother intended to do, and translate this book, and perhaps there will be other work—English lessons for the patients, or something of that sort."

There was no light in his eyes, no excitement, but he spoke in a firm voice that would hear no argument, as if describing some chore that could not be avoided.

"But... do you intend to stay there always? You can't." *I need you. I love you*, I wanted to say. But it did not matter what I needed or loved. He had no wish to be with me. He had told me so, plainly, as soon as I arrived. I had to find a reason for him to stay that concerned only him, and all I could think of was, "You have no typewriter."

"I shall hire one." He picked up his bag. "I must go. I don't want to miss this afternoon's train."

Desperate, I moved to block the doorway. "Wait a little, please, Edmund. Give me another minute or two. I shall miss you terribly—and don't you owe me an explanation, at least?"

He hesitated.

"My carriage is in the square," I went on. "I can drive you to the station. It will be quicker than taking a tram or the métro, so you can spare a few minutes before we go."

But I had pressed too hard. Edmund's brow furrowed, angry red spots appeared in his cheeks, and he gripped the door so tight that his knuckles went white.

"But that is exactly what I do *not* want you to do!" The words burst out of him. "I could make my own way to the station perfectly well, but no, you must drive me there, so that you control my time. Don't you see what you are doing? Don't you see how you take away my independence to get what you want?"

I did see. For the first time, I saw it. And I lost hope, because I had no idea how else I could keep him.

"I hate to cause you any distress," he said more gently, "but how can I avoid it? You will not let me decide anything for myself, because you always think you know best. You have never asked me what *I* want. Never once."

I racked my brain for an example to prove him wrong. "The opera. I asked if you would like to go to the opera. I did not order you to go."

"But you didn't say, 'How would you like to spend the evening, Edmund?' You offered me that opera, on that day, yes or no. I must do things your way or not at all. And you gave me money 'to make me your equal' — to try to change me, in other words. Money does not make men equals!" His voice rose, and so did the colour in his face.

"You are right about that," I said quietly. "You are the better man, and always will be. No wealth could corrupt you."

He shook his head in frustration and turned away. Some barrier had come between us, some chasm. What he said was true, but at the same time he was wrong. Yes, I had struggled to be the one who held the reins, but I had never wanted to change him. I had only wanted to give him air, a chance to grow, to be fully himself.

"So tell me what you want," I said. "Not for your brother, but for yourself, in your own life. What are your dreams?"

He stared unseeing over my shoulder. "I do not know. That is the trouble. I must go away where I can think."

A door banged, and the landlady appeared in the passageway, middle-aged and suspicious. "*Tout va bien?*"

Edmund gave her a forced smile. "Yes, madame, all is well," he said in French. "A friend has called to say goodbye."

She peered at me. "Monsieur is war-wounded? He should sit down. You may invite him into my salon."

She waved a hand further down the hall. I did not move. My world was tumbling around me, but I had to release Edmund.

"No, thank you, madame." I turned to Edmund and spoke quickly in English. "I will leave you now. I see I have thought too much of my own desires. I hoped yours were the same . . . but it is true that I never asked, and I have no wish to compel you to stay. You must have your life."

I paused, studying his face. His lips were clamped in a tight line, as if he did not trust himself to speak for fear his heart might take control of his head. He felt something, I was sure he did. But perhaps it was only pity.

I swung out into the passage. He opened the front door for me, and I manoeuvred over the threshold. "If you return those bonds to Finlayson, however," I went on, "I intend to set up a trust for Robert. You can be a trustee or not as you like, but I think you must allow me to do that for him — or at least tell him I have offered and let the decision be his."

He stared at me, then swallowed and closed his eyes for a second as if blinking back tears. His colour was slowly returning to normal. He did not speak, but he nodded acceptance.

"And I will send you my typewriter. I will have it delivered to the sanatorium."

"I—"

"Consider it a loan if you like." This was too much like something I had said about the money, so I hurried on before he could refuse. "If Claude is happy with the book, I have no more use for the machine, and you may not easily find one that has the letters arranged in the English way."

He smiled—not directly at me, but over my shoulder. "Thank you."

"Then farewell." I forced out the words. "If ever there is anything I can do for you, you know where I am. In the meantime, I wish you every happiness."

My heart ached. I hoped he would not want me to go. I yearned for him to stop me. But he only nodded again. "And the same to you, Mr. Clarynton."

When I reached the square, I looked back. He had left the house and was walking swiftly away, head down, carrying his bag—hurrying out of my life.

My heart was hollow as I handed Parkin my hat.

"We have lost him. He is going to join his brother in Switzerland, to get away from me."

"I am very sorry to hear that, sir." He helped me off with my coat and shook out the sleeves. "If you'll excuse me asking, does he understand your feelings? You're so used to putting on a brave face, he might not know—"

"He knows," I said bitterly.

Or did he? I thought back over all I had said to him in these last months. I had told him I would miss him—but that was only today, and I would say the same to Parkin if he left my service. Had I ever told Edmund how I felt?

Perhaps I had not. But it was too late. He would not believe me, however sincere I was. He would think I was only trying to stop him leaving—and of course he would be right, but—

"Well, sir, the tea tray's all ready. I'll just go and warm the pot."

Then it came to me. I did have a way to show him how I had felt all along.

I clutched at Parkin's arm. "Where is the railway timetable? What time does the train leave for Geneva?"

I did not wait for his reply but hurried to the library and pulled the railway guide from the shelf. I tore some of its flimsy pages in my haste to find the place, then glanced at my watch. Yes, there was time. He had given himself over an hour to reach the station from Auteuil. He might not even be there yet.

I shouted down the corridor. "Parkin! Will you go down and find the coachman? I want the carriage again at once."

I went to my room and took this book from its place in a drawer beside the bed. Then back to the library, where my fingers fumbled with brown paper and string.

46

James's Journal, continued

I urged the coachman to drive to the station as fast as he could. Edmund stood in the queue for the ticket office, a lonely figure in a shabby coat. His mouth dropped open when he saw me, but he did not shrink away as he had at the house.

I thrust the package at him. "Please take this."

He put down his bag, took the parcel in both hands, and turned it over. "Is it a copy of your book?"

"My— Oh! The thing on chinoiserie? No. It is my journal."

He looked at me uncertainly. I spoke fast.

"I know that by giving you this, I am only telling you again what I want, but I think perhaps you have not understood how I ... well, I cannot say what I mean in a public place, but you will know if you read this. I hope you will not be offended by the earlier parts. I did not always feel so deeply. It has come upon me slowly, and here you can see how and why and when."

The words tumbled over themselves as they spilled out of me, leaving him no pause to answer. "Will you read this in the train, or when you reach Switzerland, and then take all the time you need to decide what you want to do, and tell me? You can write or telephone — and you do not have to, you can throw the thing off a mountain when you are done if you like, and never see me again—but if you will write, if you will talk to me—and you never did, you know, it has not always been my fault, you told me so little—but what I mean is I will listen. I have a huge respect for your opinions and—and a great deal more than respect, and I will always listen."

He stared down at the parcel, frowning over it, and did not speak. People in the queue were sneaking glances at us. Possibly some of them spoke English and had understood me. Had I embarrassed him? I waited a little longer, but still he said nothing.

"Well, I... I will leave you, then." I gave him a moment more. He remained silent, so I gripped my crutches and turned away.

I stopped at the ticket hall doors. He was watching me and had not moved, although the couple ahead had advanced two or three feet. I raised my hand to bid him goodbye. His expression did not change.

I may never see him again.

Pain skewered me to the spot.

Then the man behind Edmund tapped him on the shoulder and pointed at the space in front of him. Edmund turned away from me, reached down for his bag, and stepped forward. He did not look back again.

I went home and let Parkin bring me the tea tray. I ate one jam sandwich and half a slice of cake—a nursery tea, fit for a man who felt as desolate as an orphaned child.

I put in the new eye to exercise the muscles in the socket as instructed, and Parkin helped me fit the leg, but I could get up no interest in any of it. My mind was with Edmund. By now he would be in the train, reading my deepest and darkest thoughts. What would he make of them? Passage after passage came to my memory, bringing a blush to my cheeks.

If I had reflected, I might not have given it to him. Too much of me was in it—and too much of him. I winced when I imagined him reading my first impressions of him at our interview or my talks with Claude and Diana.

But he would understand my feelings for him. He would see how they began, how they grew, and how much stronger they were than my feelings for Louis or anyone else.

He would know me. He might no longer admire but perhaps he could forgive the man he found in the pages, the man I am. Then in a few months or years we might meet again, and something new might begin.

In the meantime, those months and years stretched ahead of me like an ashen desert.

I tried to distract myself with a book, and I must have dozed. A softly closing door roused me to consciousness.

"Parkin?"

There was no answer. I opened my eyes.

Edmund stood before me, his gaze hooded, his mouth unsmiling, and the cuffs of his trousers dusty. My heart thumped. I blinked and sat up, disoriented.

"Edmund? Is it you? Is it morning? Have I slept here all night?"

His expression was blank. "No, it is about half past seven in the evening—Tuesday evening. I have brought this back to you." He showed me the parcel, still wrapped and tied with the string.

"You did not want to take it with you? You could not bring yourself to read it? But you must have missed your train."

"I did not exactly miss the train, because I did not buy a ticket. I began to read in the queue, and then I did not want to stop, so I went to the waiting room to finish it."

I looked again at the package he held in both hands. The bow was much neater than the one I had tied. "Then please tell me why you are here. Not that I am sorry to see you — on the contrary, I am happier than I can say, but I want to make no more assumptions."

His mouth twitched. Was that a smile? "You said you would like me to read it and let you know what I wanted. I have come to do that. May I sit down?"

"Of course." My voice cracked with tension.

He settled in one of the Rococo chairs, set the journal on his lap, and adjusted his trousers at the knees, all without meeting my gaze. I wanted to prompt him with *Do you want this, or do you want that?* but I made myself wait.

I must listen, I told myself. *I must truly listen to him.*

"First, as I said before, I should like to return your money. All of it." He looked at the floor as he spoke. "I do not think you need to do anything for Robby. I hope my mother's family will help. But—"

"Please believe I did not make that suggestion to create a tie with you," I interrupted. "I would do the same for the boy if you were on the other side of the world."

"Yes, I see there is some fellow-feeling between you that has nothing to do with me." He fingered the journal through its brown paper wrapping. "I will not interfere. If you truly wish to do it, then I have no objection, and I am sure he will be very grateful. I think he would want me to be a trustee, so I will accept that responsibility if you do not change your mind."

I began to assure him I would not, but he held up a hand to stop me, and I remembered I was supposed to be listening.

"I will stay in Paris for the time being, after all," he went on.

My heart jumped for joy.

"I would like to do what I intended to do in Davos: that is, begin the translation and perhaps give some private English lessons."

"I am delighted to hear it. And will you go back and live with Madame What's-her-name?"

"Huguet. I have not decided about that."

"Yes, yes, I must not tell you what to do. But my offer of the typewriter still stands, and if your room in Auteuil is cold"—but it would not be, with summer approaching—"or . . . or small, or"—inspiration struck me—"or if your typewriting and English lessons might disturb the other tenants, you are welcome to keep the machine here and treat my library as your office."

He raised his beautiful long-lashed eyes to meet mine. "You are doing it again. You are trying to make me dependent on you." But the eyes sparkled with amusement, his mouth was soft, and his voice held none of the anger he had shown me at his landlady's.

"No, I am not. I— Well, I see what you mean. But you can always challenge me, you know, as you just did. I do not mind, and you do not seem to find it difficult."

He flushed a little. "It is not difficult if you are not my employer. But thank you for the offer—I would be glad to use your library. And as Madame Huguet is not expecting me, perhaps I could stay here tonight?"

"Of course!" My cheeks ached from the unaccustomed stretch of my smile. I thought of something he had said this afternoon and dared to add, "And how would you like to spend this evening, Edmund?"

He gave a quick laugh. "You have no engagements?"

"No. I am all yours."

"Then I should like to dine with you, I think."

"Nothing would give me more pleasure. Where shall we go?"

"I mean, to dine here. Just to eat together and talk."

"Even better. I shall certainly ask you what you want to do more often, if you are as easy to please as that. Let me ring for Parkin."

I stood up and pulled the bell cord. Edmund gasped, and his face broke into a smile of pure joy.

"James, you are walking!"

A weight lifted from my shoulders. All the clouds that had troubled me were gone, blown away by a breeze of pure happiness. For how could he look so delighted at my ability to walk if he did not care for me?

"And?" I said. "Do you not notice how handsome I have become?"

He blinked, and the smile grew wider. "You have a new eye! How did I not see it before? I suppose because it does not change you. You always were handsome. Oh, but I am so happy for you!"

"Is that all you feel—happy for me?" I teased.

He gave a short laugh and looked away. "Perhaps I will let you see my journal one day, or parts of it, so you will know exactly what I feel. But it is in shorthand, so I shall have to read it to you, and that would take time."

"We have time. We shall have all the time we want."

"Yes. Oh, James..."

He came closer. To my astonishment, he kissed me on the lips, a sweet, lingering kiss. But he still clasped this book with both hands, and it made a barrier between us. I reached for it.

He snatched it away. "No, you may not have it back yet! There are parts I want to read again. I did not know whether to laugh or cry at the station. It made me do both. Sometimes you have been so sly!"

But he was laughing, so I grasped the parcel and pulled. He played at struggling, his body supple and warm against mine, as if he wanted to run from me. But it was only pretence. He could have knocked me over with ease.

I had grasped Edmund's arm, with my other hand on the journal, when he twisted around, snatching the book back. I stumbled, and the false leg grated against my stump. A cry of pain escaped me.

Parkin chose that moment to come in.

We broke apart. I tried to calm my racing heart and appear the sober gentleman, but I could not remove the smile that split my face in two.

"Now, sir," Parkin said to Edmund, "you won't forget his leg."

"Your leg!" Edmund's free hand went to his mouth in horror. "Is it hurt?"

"No." I patted his shoulder, but I was careful not to put my weight on that side. "At least, it was not your fault. It needs a rest now, perhaps. I shall sit down, and you might be kind enough to fetch my crutches while Parkin helps me off with this thing."

"I am so sorry, James!"

Parkin saw to my leg, and I told him we would be two for dinner. When he had gone, smiling to himself, I said to Edmund, "Now will you let me have my journal?"

Edmund held it closer to his chest and kept his distance. "I do not want to give it up."

"I will show you the place in my room where I keep it, and you may come in and read it whenever you like."

"Very well." He put down the journal on the table where he used to take dictation.

In the silence that followed, my heart beat as loud as the drums of Africa. All seemed well between us, but a knot of stress still disturbed my happiness. I needed his reassurance.

"You will stay in Paris, then? And . . . perhaps you will stay with me?"

"Yes, I believe I will. I don't know how I ever thought I could leave." He laughed. "I was so jealous of Louis!"

"You had no reason to be."

He came closer, hesitated, and sat on the couch beside me. His scent filled my nostrils, a delicate mixture of soap, ink, wool, and masculinity. I had not known how much I missed it until that moment.

"You see now that the affair with Louis ended long ago?" I asked. "He had not spent a night here since before I knew you."

"Yes, but that was not the question, or not all of it. He'd had your—your affection, and I had not. I was afraid I never would."

Claude had once advised me to speak what was in my heart, and now was the moment to do it. I looked into Edmund's eyes.

"No, you are wrong. The opposite is true. You have my affection and more. You have my love, and he never had that. As for the enjoyment of it, you have not had much of that yet, but you will. Here is a taste." And I bent my head to caress his lips with mine.

We dressed for dinner. Edmund wore the new suit he had left in the wardrobe here. He said nothing about it and nor did I, except to compliment him on his appearance.

It was not the festive meal I had planned on Sunday, because it was Henri's day off. Parkin brought us the assortment of dishes I had not touched while Edmund was missing. They made an odd collation, but we did not care. I would not have cared if there had been only bread and butter. We teased and laughed and sat close together, feeding each other with our fingers. Edmund seemed as comfortable in his new clothes as he had in the old, and I . . . I felt my life was transformed.

This morning, when Parkin came in, I was not alone. Edmund slept beside me, with one arm thrown across my chest.

Parkin showed no surprise. He put my tea on the bedside table, went out, and returned a moment later with a second cup, for Edmund.

"You may open the shutters," I murmured.

He pushed them back quietly. Edmund did not stir. Outside, the sky was the clear blue of a summer lake.

"I have closed myself up in this apartment too long, Parkin."

"Yes, sir."

"Now the doctors are finished with me, we are thinking of taking a house in the country."

My servant paused for a moment in mid-step, then recovered himself. "I'm sure that will do you the world of good, Mr. Clarynton."

Mr. Clarynton, not *sir*—it was a warning. He would give notice if I left Paris. He would not be separated from his butler.

I watched him until he was almost at the door. Barely a muscle twitched to show how perturbed he must be.

I smiled to myself. Edmund and I had discussed this over dinner, during one of Parkin's long, tactful absences from the dining room.

"We shall want a butler, Parkin, a discreet man who has had enough of the hurly-burly of the city and would appreciate a quiet life. Might you know of someone?"

He lifted his head. The tension went out of his shoulders and a smile flickered across that impassive face. "I'll see what I can do, sir."

He left the room, and Edmund woke . . .

47

James's Journal
Plessy-les-Bois, Thursday, August 28th

Parkin insisted on clearing the west bedroom in preparation for Diana's visit next week, and I found this book at the bottom of a trunk. I shall add a few lines now, while Parkin hunts for rugs and bed linen, then return it to the trunk and consign it to the attic.

For I have no wish to continue this journal. I began it to give me an interest in life, and I have found one much greater, an interest that lives and breathes and, impossible as it seems, loves me. To Edmund I tell all the things I would have written. To him I speak my heart.

A great deal has happened since last I wrote. The apartment has been covered in dust sheets, and we have moved to the country, where we will stay until the cold weather begins to bite.

We had looked at perhaps ten or twelve properties when we came upon this place some fifty miles from Paris. It is not far from a station, and the nearest junction away connects us with the main line to Switzerland. Last month we were able to visit Robby, after some argument about the financing of the trip. In the end, Robby's trust paid Edmund's fares.

The boy seems better, although as he once told me, one can get better without getting well. He has some way to go, certainly, but the doctors say there is hope.

The local people call this house a chateau, but it is a small one, no bigger than an ordinary English manor house or large rectory—the perfect size for two gentlemen who want to live quietly together, with room for a grand piano, a library, and occasional guests.

It is pleasing to the eye, built of red brick with white stone copings and a turreted roof. Outside, beyond the house, the stables, the orchard, and the kitchen garden, there is a large pond and a half-wild flower garden in the English style.

Edmund fell for it at first sight.

"Oh, James, I believe this is the one. I see now what the voice meant, when it told me I was in the wrong place. It was not a choice of in Paris with you, or away from Paris without you. This is the right place—with you, and away from Paris."

I did not know what he meant at the time, but I saw that we must have the house. I cannot say no to him when his eyes light up with enthusiasm.

Parkin fussed about the unsuitable sanitary arrangements, but his butler, *our* butler, Williams, has proved himself more than capable of persuading the local tradesmen to modernise the plumbing. Indeed, he is so capable that I sometimes wish for the days when there was only Parkin to answer bells and see to all my needs. But Parkin now has the extensive wardrobes of two young gentlemen to manage, not to mention all the other accoutrements of living in the country. And as if there weren't enough of those —

"Diana insists on bringing me one of her husband's first motor cars," I grumbled to Edmund last evening. "I hadn't thought there could be any danger of that yet, but it seems he has gone in with someone who is already producing them. I told her no — quite firmly — but she is driving over in it anyway, and she says I can try it out during her visit. I do not know how she thinks I can control the thing with one leg."

"Our gardener drove ambulances during the war," Edmund reminded me. "She can be our chauffeur."

The gardener came with the cook that Williams found for us when Henri refused to leave his large family in Paris. I had taken on my new employees before it fully sank in that both cook and gardener were females. I did not want women fussing and gossiping and interfering with our way of life. However, these women are not that sort. They live quietly together in the gardener's cottage and never trespass upon the upstairs part of our house.

"And perhaps she will teach *me* to drive," Edmund added, with the same light in his eyes that he had when we first saw this house.

So my fate is sealed. I am about to become the owner of a motor car.

It may be no bad thing. On our recent excursions, I have begun to see their advantages. Horses seem much slower in the country, where the distances are greater.

I have told Diana nothing about Edmund in my letters. She knows he is here, but she thinks he is still no more than my secretary. She will have to spend time with us to understand that I have not corrupted him, whatever our relations may be.

Indeed, I believe that nothing could corrupt him. He has a strength that neither Diana nor I could see in Paris all those months ago.

My love for him grows every day. I even begin to understand why men marry . . .

And here he is now, wanting me to go to the orchard to see if the apples are ripe. On the way, no doubt, we will stop at the corner of the garden that he has made beautiful in memory of his mother. He has no hesitation in taking me there. He says that if she is looking down on us, she will not mind.

Suicide Prevention

If you have suicidal thoughts or know someone who does, please seek help. The thoughts are more likely to stop with counselling or treatment.

You'll find links to international helplines at this site:

suicideprevention.wikia.com/wiki/International_Suicide_Prevention_Directory

Acknowledgements

I'd like to thank everyone who has helped and encouraged me through the writing and polishing of this book, and in particular:

- Sandra E. Sinclair, who reads my first drafts and has winkled me out of despondencies almost as deep as my characters' on more occasions than I can count;

- Carole-ann Galloway, whose eagle eyes and helpful suggestions have made this a much smoother reading experience than it was when it first left my hands;

- and of course my friends and family, headed by my long-suffering parents, who have supported me through thick and thin (mostly thin), without judging and often without having a clue what I was doing. Thanks, folks!

This book was inspired by a story by Elinor Glyn (1864-1943). Both she and her romantic fiction were considered scandalous a hundred years ago, so I hope that, like Edmund's mother, if she is looking down on us, she will not mind.

About the Author

Megan Reddaway has been entertained by fictional characters acting out their stories in her head for as long as she can remember. She began writing them down as soon as she could.

Since she grew up, she has worked as a secretary, driver, barperson, and marketer, among other things. Whatever she is doing, she always has a story bubbling away at the same time.

She lived in France for fourteen months around the turn of the millennium and speaks French fast, but not accurately. She now lives in England.

Website (with free stories, *The Luck of the Irish* and *Wrong Number*, if you sign up to her newsletter):
meganreddaway.com

Facebook Page:
facebook.com/meganreddawayauthor/

Goodreads:
goodreads.com/author/show/5753619.Megan_Reddaway

Twitter:
twitter.com/meganreddaway1

Also by Megan Reddaway

Shelter Me

Gay romance in a not-so-distant future

Love and survival — is it too much to ask?

Leo Park is an empath on the run. He's escaped the secret research facility where he's been held since he was six years old, but how can he survive without being captured? He has no money, all his ideas come from old movies, and he's carrying his baby brother, smuggled out in a carton.

Cole Millard lives by his own rules in the Oregon woods, refusing to fear the world war that's coming closer every day. Now his freedom is threatened by a naive 19-year-old with a baby in tow and a spooky way of knowing what Cole is feeling. But Leo is vulnerable and desperate. What's a guy to do?

***Shelter Me** is a dystopian gay romance novel with a hot backwoodsman, a desperate fugitive, a six-month-old baby, and the world on the brink of an apocalyptic war.*

Big Guy

A sweet and funny gay romance novella

Overweight Truman Rautigan and his mom are about to be made homeless, but she's a top slimming salesperson who could win her dream house if Truman comes through with some sales of his own. Instead, he's stashing food in his bottom drawer and indulging in late-night binges.

When his mom sends him to infiltrate a rival weight loss group, he meets the gorgeous Brad, biker, mechanic and successful slimmer. But Brad couldn't be interested in Truman, could he? What if he knew Truman's real reason for being there? Truman could lose everything if his shameful secrets are exposed…

Out, Proud, and Prejudiced
A *modern retelling of Jane Austen's* Pride and Prejudice

One's proud, one's prejudiced, and they can't stand each other.

Quick-tempered Bennet Rourke dislikes Darius Lanniker on sight. Darius may be a hotshot city lawyer, but that doesn't give him the right to sneer at Bennet, his friends, and their college. It doesn't help that Bennet's restaurant job has him waiting at Darius's table. So when his tutor recommends him for an internship at Darius's Pemberley estate, Bennet isn't sure he wants it. He's also not sure he can afford to turn it down.

Darius is a fish out of water in the small college town of Meriton, but something keeps pulling him back there. He's helping out a friend with business advice, nothing more. If he's interested in Bennet, it's not serious. Sure, Bennet challenges him in a way no other man has. But they have nothing in common. Right?

Wrong. Their best friends are falling in love, and Bennet and Darius can't seem to escape each other. Soon they're sharing climbing ropes and birthday cake, and there's a spark between them that won't be denied.

But betrayal is around the corner. Darius must swallow his pride and Bennet must drop his prejudices to see the rainbow shining through the storm clouds.